HORSEMEN ON THE HILLS

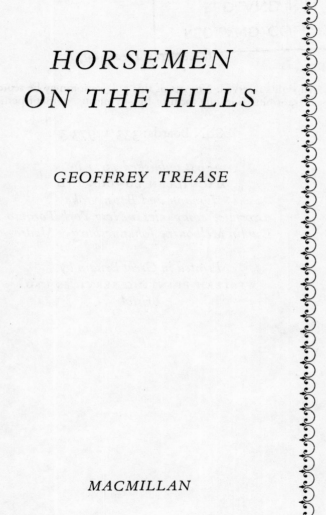

HORSEMEN ON THE HILLS

GEOFFREY TREASE

MACMILLAN

YF

© *Geoffrey Trease 1971*

SBN Boards: 333 12973 3

First published 1971 by
MACMILLAN LONDON LTD
London and Basingstoke
Associated companies in New York Toronto
Dublin Melbourne Johannesburg & Madras

Printed in Great Britain by
WESTERN PRINTING SERVICES LTD
Bristol

For Penelope

For Pandora

Contents

Contents

CHAPTER ONE

Reflections in a Lake

THAT first time, he took her for another boy.

He lay floating idly, deliciously, his hair trailing like dark weed in water warmed by long days of sun, now and then shifting slightly in the current that stole invisibly through the placid lake.

His own turn in the saddle was over. The sweat was washed away, the aching muscles eased. The world was all evening freshness.

Now the last line of young riders was defiling along the strand between the reedy margin and the swallow-tailed battlements of the Castello. The boys rode slowly, intent on dressage and deportment, aware that the Marquis himself was watching. They made living sculpture, a frieze of docile centaurs, matching their own upside-down images in the lagoon.

It was the sudden noise, the urgent drumming of hastier hoofs, that made him raise his head and stare.

One rider was thundering along, far behind the others, as though anxious to close the gap between him and the rest of the string. "Him", thought Sandro, and "him" too thought the Marquis evidently, for he roared like an exploding bombard, his voice echoing from the brick ramparts behind.

"Stop! What are you playing at, you young devil?"

The slow-stepping pageant froze. Every rider looked back. Sandro and the other swimmers, like a shoal of fishes impelled by common instinct, drew closer to the shore. The fringe of reeds was handy. They could watch and listen without drawing the Marquis's fire upon themselves.

The galloping hoofs slowed to a halt. A girl's voice rang clear. "I am sorry, my lord –"

"*Caterina!*"

"I didn't mean to ride him so hard, my lord. He – he rather took control. But I wanted to catch up with the others."

"Lucky you weren't thrown! What should I have told your father? What's more to the point, though, what do you mean by riding out with the boys?"

"I thought – well, Master Vittorino says that a balanced education –"

"*Balanced education?*"

Again the Marquis went off like some alarming piece of siege-artillery. But this time, Sandro noticed, there was more good humour in the explosive mixture. Peeping cautiously between the tasselled reeds, he gained his first close view of the girl and remembered vaguely that she, and one or two others, had been sitting on the bench at the back of the school-room earlier in the day. Only now, though, was he made aware of her as an individual.

She was no older than himself. She sat the steaming charger with remarkable serenity, straddling him under the folds of her hitched-up gown. She too was a chestnut, her bright hair rolled up under a silver net. She looked down an elegant young nose at the man who held her bridle.

"Master Vittorino says that you wish us all to have a balanced education, mind, body and spirit," she explained patiently. "Books aren't everything. There must be music, painting, gymnastics, riding – the aim is the all-round man –"

"But not the all-round woman!"

"Surely that follows, my lord? If you are going to admit girls to the school? Or can something be good and true in some cases, but bad and false in others?"

"You mustn't cross-examine *me*, child. You are not Socrates."

"But Master Vittorino told us that we must always ask questions! It is the Platonic method."

What a girl, thought Sandro with a shiver of admiration, taking on the Marquis himself! But the great Lord of Mantua, though he snorted like one of his own beloved horses, seemed more amused than anything.

"You're as bad as Cecilia. One word from me, and, father or no father, she lets fly with a flood of Greek. Plato and Demosthenes rolled into one. But even she does not take a war-horse from the stables and ride out after the lads."

"She should never need to handle a war-horse. I may."

The Marquis ignored this. "Ride on then, but carefully, for God's sake. And no more of this. I'll speak to Master Vittorino. We must find a way to balance your education without breaking your neck. I beg your pardon – you ride well, but this isn't a horse for a young girl. I'll walk back to the stables with you."

"Thank you, my lord."

The voices and jingle of harness faded. Another voice, close to Sandro's ear, commented: "A lively little piece!"

Startled, Sandro turned. One of the older boys had swum unnoticed to his side. "Er – ?" he began uncertainly.

"I said, she's a lively little piece. Caterina Spinelli."

The youth smacked his lips in a way that Master Vittorino would certainly have said was vulgar.

Sandro recognised him as Taddeo Tregani. Taddeo had spoken to him after dinner. He had gone out of his way to be friendly, but Sandro, though he needed friends badly enough, had been put off by something in his manner. Now, stripped of his elegant dress, Taddeo was even less attractive. He reminded Sandro of the wicked-looking satyr, coarse-featured and shaggy, on the great silver wine-bowl in his father's shop.

Taddeo seemed bent on making conversation.

"If she means to do *everything* the boys do, she's in for a strenuous time. Fencing, wrestling. . ." He paused and chuckled. "Come to that, though, I wouldn't mind taking her on at wrestling myself. In a year or two."

He was waiting for Sandro to make the right giggling reply. Sandro had no desire to make enemies in this new, entrancing, yet somewhat alarming world he had just entered. He pretended not to understand.

"It's turning chilly," he said. "I'm going to get some clothes on."

He struck out, ruffling the mother-of-pearl surface, eager to lose himself among the other dark bobbing heads, the pale glistening shoulders. He could feel Taddeo's eyes behind him, transfixing him with sudden dislike.

A pity. But it couldn't be helped.

CHAPTER TWO

The Happy House

AT that date Sandro was really young. Later, looking back, he realised that he had never previously thought about girls. Even that glimpse of Caterina Spinelli was – though it seemed hard to believe, in after years – pushed into the background by all the other impressions jostling in his mind on that first day.

There was, to begin with, Master Vittorino himself.

Sandro had seen him before, of course, often enough. All Mantua knew that small figure in the sombre gown, flitting like a merry bat along the arcaded streets, a smile almost always lighting the face under the peaked hood.

He had heard too – who hadn't? – the legends of the great scholar's early struggles. Vittorino da Feltre had been a penniless student in Padua. He'd worked as a servant for the mathematics professor in the hope of free tuition. When the professor declined to help him, Vittorino had doggedly set to and mastered mathematics by himself. Long after that, when he was over forty, he had been seized with a passion to learn Greek. Few people in Italy knew the language, but Vittorino was determined to find a teacher. Men were just realising how much of the wisdom of the ancients was locked up in those precious manuscripts handed down from the Greeks, and it was there for all who had troubled to acquire the key.

Vittorino had had to go to Venice and study under the renowned Guarino. Finally, ten years ago, famous himself by then, he had been persuaded to settle in Mantua as tutor to the children of the Marquis and his friends. Gradually the group had expanded, and ever since he could remember Sandro had heard stories of the wonderful school carried on inside the walls of the Castello, which now drew pupils from every corner of Italy and even from foreign countries.

It was common talk what Vittorino had done for the Marquis's own children. Lodovico Gonzaga, a lazy lump of a boy, had slimmed down and become a healthy and intelligent young man. Carlo's skinny physique had been properly developed. Their sister, Cecilia, now staggered learned visitors with her fluency in Greek. Margherita and the other younger ones were shaping well. No wonder the Marquis had confidence in Vittorino and gave him a free hand. The scholar had been allotted a separate villa within the palace precincts, where he could practise his teaching methods and create a separate little world for his pupils that would have gladdened Plato himself.

Vittorino insisted on full control. He not only laid down the timetable of study and exercise, he dictated the simple meals, allowing no luxury, and planned the whole waking day. He cared nothing for rank; he was indifferent to money. If a boy was hopelessly idle or stupid, out he went. If he had brains, however poor his family, he was given a free place. So long as the fees of the rich kept the accounts in balance, Vittorino gave his mind to more important things.

"You will be happy here," he promised Sandro that first morning. "You know what we call this place? *La Giocosa*, 'the Happy House'. So it is. Praise achieves more than punishment. But –" he paused and his lively eyes twinkled – "I am human and I have a temper. I warn all the boys; if you see me starting to lose it, make a diversion – ask me some sensible question, and set me on a different tack."

The day had passed quickly. There had been the introduction to Greek, the doorway that led to Homer and the other poets Sandro had heard mentioned always with bated breath, the playwrights, the historians, the philosophers, all those immortal authors who towered above the writers of today. Sandro had to begin at the beginning, pink tongue-tip between white teeth in furious concentration, quill firmly gripped, tracing the strangely beautiful new letters, *alpha*, *beta*, *gamma*, *delta* and the rest.

When it came to Latin he was more at home. He was already good at the language. That was how he had won his place in the school. But it was something quite fresh to be taught by Master Vittorino and catch fire from his enthusiasm.

"Do you realise, my young friends, living here in Mantua you are walking on holy ground? Virgil may have stood on this very spot. Mantua was *his* city, fifteen hundred years ago. Our river, which we call Mincio, is the same Minicius we read of in his verses, *its broad meanders fringed with nodding reeds*. He was the greatest of the Roman poets – and when he was your age he lived here."

Vittorino could not be everywhere at once. There were too many pupils, big and small. He had other teachers to help with the music and painting, just as, in the afternoon, the Marquis and his gentlemen took over the riding and fencing lessons and the various sports. But Vittorino's spirit pervaded the whole place with a sort of human sunshine.

That first day was a full one for Sandro. He was not

15

sorry when, after supper and an hour of free time, a bell sent them trooping upstairs.

He was less pleased when, as he stood fumbling with the laces of his doublet, he saw Taddeo Tregani coming down the long twilit room between the rows of beds.

He knew a little more about Taddeo by now. The youth came from Perugia. His family, he was fond of telling everybody, was one of the oldest and noblest in that famous city. Unfortunately, they had been driven out in a revolution and were living in exile as best they could. The boys who had murmured this information to Sandro did not express much sympathy for the Tregani misfortunes. They hinted that, if the rest of the family were anything like Taddeo, the people of Perugia had shown excellent taste.

The young exile stopped in front of Sandro, hand elegantly on hip, looking him up and down like some new addition to the stables. When at last he spoke, his voice had lost the smooth friendliness it had exuded earlier.

"You – what did you say your name was?"

"Alessandro Vettori."

"Vettori? I thought so. Your father's the merchant near the market-place?"

"Yes."

"I saw your efforts at fencing this afternoon. *Very* amusing." Sandro felt his cheeks warming. It had been his first lesson. The Marquis had encouraged him, said he shaped well. But Taddeo now raised his voice so that it carried halfway down the room. "Not that it really matters," he went on. "Merchants don't need fencing. They only have to sell the swords. It's the gentlemen who use them."

Sandro was stung, and he was meant to be.

"We're all equal here while we're in the school. Master Vittorino says so."

"And you take every word he says as Holy Writ?"

"No." Sandro had already absorbed the master's guiding principle: every one, everything, must be open to question. "But this is his school. He runs it his way."

"An odd way, sometimes." Taddeo changed his tack. "So you're sleeping here too?"

"Yes." Sandro nearly added, "Do you mind?" But Taddeo was a hefty youth. Better not give him an excuse to turn nasty.

"I'd have thought you could have gone home and slept over the shop?"

"My father offered. But Master Vittorino likes complete charge."

"Well, at least your *mother* won't miss you." Taddeo put such a weight of meaning into his apparently casual remark that he drew all eyes and ears upon them. Boys stood, their hose unrolled about their knees, their fingers motionless on half-unfastened laces.

"No," Sandro muttered. He stooped and arranged his shoes, very neatly, beside his bed. The evening light was draining fast from the room but he was glad of the excuse to turn away his face.

"In fact," Taddeo persisted remorselessly, "Mistress Maria Vettori isn't your mother at all, is she?" Sandro made no answer. "Your mother was a servant-girl at an inn in Verona – your father used to stay there on his business journeys – so you are not even his legitimate son –"

"You seem to know all about it." Sandro straightened up and faced him. His words came out huskily. "But it's an old story. Plenty of people in Mantua know. Even an – an outsider – can learn these things. If he listens to gossip." He was past caring now. If Taddeo laid hands on him he would fight back, hopeless though it might be.

"Are you calling me an outsider?"

The long room had grown very silent.

Only one person moved. Light footsteps came down between the beds. Sandro dared not take his eyes off Taddeo, but he was aware of the other boy's approach. The figure loomed at his elbow. A senior, though not as tall as the Perugian. A voice said, pleasantly – really pleasantly:

"*My* father too had his love-affairs. Which makes me what our friend Taddeo would call a bastard. Do you want a general discussion on the subject, Taddeo?"

"I wasn't referring to you."

Taddeo turned and walked away to his own end of the room. "Good night, young Sandro," said the other boy. "Sleep well. And don't worry about *him*." He followed Taddeo.

CHAPTER THREE

The Hostage

Not until next morning could Sandro learn much about the boy who had cut short Taddeo's interrogation.

Federigo was from the Marches, the mountain country to the south. His father was a Montefeltro, Count of Urbino. No one knew his mother's name; she'd been some local girl who had caught his lordship's questing eye. The usual story. But, though Federigo had been born outside lawful wedlock, he had status as the Count's acknowledged son, and he had spent his childhood in the palace at Urbino along with his legitimate young half-brother.

A boy said, "Federigo's really here as a hostage."

"Why?"

"The Count, his father, had some trouble with Venice. It was part of the settlement. Federigo was sent to Venice as a guarantee that Montelfeltro would keep his word."

"Then what's he doing in Mantua?"

"It was the plague in Venice last year. They were afraid he'd catch it and die on them. They handed him over to the Marquis – he is an ally of the Venetians, after all. They knew Federigo would be safe with him."

So Federigo was a kind of prisoner. It did not seem to worry him. He had become a popular figure. He was nothing special to look at, just a dark-haired, olive-skinned boy with a friendly mouth and humorous eyes.

"But oh, he's a charmer."

Some one, Sandro could never remember who, said that and laid his finger on Federigo's outstanding quality.

In Venice, the report ran, he had charmed every one, even the mighty Doge. The Venetian youths had clubs, wearing hose of different colours as their uniform: they had all wanted Federigo as a member. Now in Mantua it was the same. He was liked because he never put on airs, though he was good at most things and utterly fearless in every branch of sport.

Perhaps he was good at things, Sandro speculated, because he always seemed interested: the all-round boy, just the material Master Vittorino wanted for his all-round man. Even in the painting and modelling lessons Federigo was a persistent questioner, ever striving to solve technical problems. Some of the grander pupils sniffed at these subjects. What was the sense of messing about with paints and clay? They were not going to earn a living as craftsmen. Presumably Federigo wasn't either, yet to see him in the art classes you might have thought he had no other aim in life.

On the first Sunday Sandro dutifully went home. "Honour thy father and thy mother," Master Vittorino reminded him a little tactlessly. He quoted the Scriptures as often as the Classics. He could not be expected to remember that it was not his mother Sandro would be visiting, and that Mistress Vettori might not have been altogether heart-broken if the boy had stayed away.

"This Federigo," said Giovanni Vettori when dinner was over, "so far you have babbled of no one but Federigo. Who is he?"

Sandro explained at length.

"H'm," said his father, disappointed. "Urbino? A poor place. Not much there."

"And *he* won't inherit it, anyhow." Mistress Vettori pursed her lips over her embroidery. "Since you say there are legitimate children." She never let Sandro forget his position in her home.

"Mother means," said young Francesco, "this hero of yours isn't worth wasting much time on."

"Wasting time?" Sandro protested in a puzzled tone.

Francesco was fifteen, and very knowing since he had started training in his father's counting-house. "If you go to this fancy school," he explained, "you're expected to make the sort of friends who'll be useful later on – useful to all of us. People who'll have money to spend, big money, and who'll come to us to spend it –"

"That will do, Francesco." Their father spoke sharply and there was a flush in his cheeks not solely due to the wine at dinner. "Sandro is going to Master Vittorino's school because he has brains and a bent for learning."

"An obsession," muttered Mistress Vettori disapprovingly.

Her husband glanced at her, but thought it best to ignore the interruption. "I may be only a man of business. God does not make us all alike – but I am proud that any son of mine – *any* son – should be a scholar. Of course, Sandro will mix with boys of good family, and some of these boys will be men of importance when they grow up. Am I to be sorry about that?" He snorted indignantly. "But nothing was further from my thoughts when I let him go there."

With a slightly sick feeling Sandro recognised the insincerity in his father's voice. He had often heard it in the shop below, when some well-to-do customer was being talked into an expensive purchase. Giovanni Vettori did not often lie; he just did not tell the truth. It was not smart to lie, for liars became known sooner or later and customers were lost. But there was a middle ground, between outright falsehood and complete frankness, and that was where the profits were made.

His father was genuinely proud and pleased that his son had been picked out to attend Master Vittorino's school. But, however much lip-service he paid to ideals of learning, he was still one of the shrewdest merchants in Mantua. It wasn't in his nature to forget the advantages of having a son who hobnobbed with the children of the Marquis and other people of that class.

Susannna, too small to be interested in these awkward undercurrents of the conversation, piped up conveniently:

"Is it true that there are girls in Master Vittorino's school?"

"A few."

"Now that is something I *don't* agree with," said Mistress Vettori as if she agreed with most things, which in Sandro's experience was far from true. "A girl needs enough schooling to keep her household accounts straight, but she doesn't want to fill her head with all this book-learning. Not unless you mean to make a nun of her."

"It's different for great ladies," said the merchant. "The Marquis wanted his daughters to learn with their brothers. That started it. Now the other gentlefolk must copy him."

"Fashion!" said Mistress Vettori scornfully, jabbing her needle into the helpless material.

The merchant laughed. "We'd be badly off without fashion, my love. Fashion keeps the goods moving."

Can they talk of nothing but money and profits? Sandro thought. A week ago it would not have bothered him. He had grown up in this atmosphere. But a few days with

Master Vittorino had opened windows in his mind, shown him wider views and revealed another world.

"What are the girls like?" pursued Susanna. "What are their names?"

Sandro told her as much as he knew, which was not much. There were only three girls of his own age. One was Margherita Gonzaga, the Marquis's youngest daughter. There was Anna – he wasn't sure of her full name – a mouselike little creature from Ferrara. And, he tried hard to sound casual, there was Caterina Spinelli. She came, he believed, from the Marches, like Federigo.

"Never mind Federigo. What's *she* like? Is she pretty?"

"I – I suppose so. I haven't really thought. Truly, Susanna, I've scarcely noticed. They sit together at the back, they keep to themselves."

"I should hope so," said Mistress Vettori, severely. "And see you take care, Sandro." She gave him a dour look. "Don't speak to them unless they speak to you. Remember who you are and what you are. The Marquis may have odd ideas, but he's no fool, depend on it. He'll draw the line fast enough if you get too familiar."

"That's right," her husband agreed. "By all means make friends with the boys – you can't have too many friends – but steer clear of the young ladies. One word amiss, one look even – you'll be out on your ear. And that teacher won't be able to save you, however much Greek you can spout."

"I'm not interested in the girls, Father –"

"Time will change that."

"Your father knows what he's talking about," said Mistress Vettori waspishly, and Sandro saw his father wince.

It was always the same. The house was full of tensions.

His stepmother – she wasn't even strictly his stepmother, but how else could he think of her? – resented his presence, indeed his very existence. She knew that men were often faithless, that children were born to them by other women, and that such children were commonly brought up in their father's house. Great ladies had to put up with the situation, but no wife, high or low, could be expected to like it. So Mistress Vettori relieved her feelings with constant digs at her husband, never letting him forget the wrong he had done her with his goings-on in other cities.

Sandro could not entirely blame her. He was growing up fast. Already he had a glimmering of the way the adult mind worked, the odd things men and women did, the emotions that impelled them to action and reaction. He understood his stepmother's resentment.

For himself it was bad luck. He had not asked to be born. And it was natural for her to be jealous when his father showed affection for him. She was anxious for her own brood. Who could blame her? Anything given to Sandro was that much less for Francesco, Susanna and the other children. A mother must look after her own.

Though he had looked forward to this visit home, he was not sorry when a nearby church bell reminded him that it was time to say goodbye. In this tall dark house above the shop, in this narrow ravine-like street running off the Piazza dell'Erbe, there were altogether too many cross-currents. His father's divided affections tugging this way and that, Mistress Vettori's anxious insecurity, her children's mixed feelings for their half-brother . . . Lucky, thought Sandro with a wry smile, that there were not so many cross-currents in the lake, or he would have drowned long ago.

He reached the piazza and turned in the direction of

the Castello. An archway led through to the other big square, the Piazza di San Pietro. High above it, clamped to the brickwork of a lofty tower, hung a great iron cage. Sometimes men who had been guilty of some particularly dire crime were put into it until, after long agonies of hunger and thirst, they died. He remembered once hearing the pitiful cries of one such prisoner, and he never passed beneath the cage without a shudder. Ordinarily, the Piazza dell'Erbe was a cheerful enough place, where, tomorrow morning, they would be setting out the stalls again and the air would quiver with haggling voices. This was the materialist, down-to-earth world in which he had grown up.

Quite different was the world beyond the archway. The other piazza had serenity, dignity, nobility. It stretched away in the mellow evening sunshine, flanked with palaces, to San Pietro's church at the far end and the lofty bell-tower golden against the sky. It led to the Castello. And beyond the Castello drawbridge, set amid all the elegance and magnificence of the fortress like some jewel in its casket, was the "Happy House" of Master Vittorino, a treasury of knowledge and ideas and talk and activity.

How good it was to be among the boys again at the supper-table! He was accepted here. There were no tensions. So long as he kept out of Taddeo Tregani's way, he found everywhere an easy friendliness.

In one way, in fact, he had won instant popularity. His fellow students had discovered that he was a born story-teller. In the past, at home, told to keep the younger children quiet, he had found that the simplest way was to amuse them with fantastic tales, blending inventions of his own with what he remembered from books. Now, to his amazement, this natural gift proved an immediate success with the boys at the school.

25

Story-telling became his regular bedtime duty, an unofficial part of the day's programme unknown to the teachers. Federigo would give the word. "Now, young Sandro! Story, please!" And down both sides of the long room all the boys would leap out of their beds again and gather round, for all the world like the naked souls resurrected in some great painting of Judgment Day.

That Sunday evening Sandro was in good form. He told them a story of battles and sieges and wild escapes, piling adventure upon adventure while they hung on his words. Then he surprised them with a happy ending none of them had foreseen.

Federigo laughed with delight. "You get better and better, Sandrino! I'll tell you what: if I ever grow up to become a famous general, you shall come on all my campaigns and write up the history of my mighty victories!"

"That's a commission," said Sandro.

"He has one excellent qualification for it," said Taddeo Tregani with a sneer. "He is a natural liar."

CHAPTER FOUR

Caterina

"I wish," said Caterina, "that babies were born in litters.
Like puppies."

"Oh, *really*!" Anna exclaimed in her most pious tone.
That girl, thought Caterina crossly, made almost a profession of sounding shocked.

"It would certainly simplify matters in some ways," said
Margherita Gonzaga, brown head aslant, peering into her
hand-mirror for reassurance that she truly had inherited
the family good looks. You could not trust compliments
when you were the Marquis's daughter. You might be
hideous: people would still gush and call you a beautiful
child. Moderately satisfied with what she saw, she turned
her mind back to her friend's problems. "What were you
thinking of, particularly?"

Caterina was staring moodily through the window of
the bedroom the three girls shared. There were fishing
boats on the Middle Lake. The waterwheels were spin-
ning round; she could hear the rhythmic clack from the
dozen mills on the covered causeway dividing the two
lagoons. In the distance the vast plain faded away and
away into a final blurred blueness. This long view, out
across the battlements, made it worth climbing all those
stairs. It was the nearest you could get to the feeling of
standing on a hill-top at home.

27

"If people had children at all," she answered slowly, "the chances would be they'd have one boy, anyhow, mixed with the girls."

"Oh that again! Don't give up. You may have a brother even yet."

"Mother will have no more children. They've prayed, they've vowed this and that, they've made pilgrimages, they've asked doctors, they've consulted the stars. Father will never have a son. Unless, of course –" Caterina hesitated, then forced herself to finish. "Unless anything should happen to Mother."

"What a thing to say!" Anna crossed herself.

"I'm only listing possibilities." Caterina spun round. "Do you imagine I like thinking about it?"

"It seems dreadful even to mention it," said Anna primly, "worse to *discuss* it."

"In this school we discuss everything." Involuntarily Caterina fell into her usual affectionate mimicry of Master Vittorino. Margherita laughed, but stopped abruptly. After all, this was a painful subject for her friend. Caterina went on: "Father would be sure to marry again. He'd feel it was his duty." The others said nothing. She was probably right.

Caterina turned again, leant her elbows on the hard sill, and stared across the lakes, homesick for the Marches where, on clear days, you could see pale slivers of the Adriatic gleaming between the gaps of hump-backed hills.

San Stefano – home – seemed another world. The little town, perched on its crag like a nesting bird, was in a sort of no-man's-land. Seaward lay the territory of the ferocious Malatestas; inland the Montefeltro family – Federigo's people – were lords of the hill country. San Stefano was a Montefeltro town, but the Malatestas had once held it and might grab it again. On the border-line between two such jealous neighbours her father needed the nerve of a tight-rope walker.

"When you see strange horsemen on the hills," he would say, "it's a sure sign of storm. A wise man bolts his door."

She was old enough to understand. It meant raiders, a signal for the country people to crowd into San Stefano with their cattle and possessions.

Her father had another favourite saying, "San Stefano needs a man," but this made her curl up inside, in shame for herself and her mother. From her earliest years she had known the bitter truth; that she was a disappointment, however hard he tried to conceal it. So was her mother. She had borne him no son, and two hundred years of Spinelli lordship seemed fated to peter out like a stream in summer drought.

When younger she had pretended to herself that somehow she could defy Nature and take on the role of that brother she would never have. She listened hungrily to tales of famous women who had held their own in a world of violent men, women like Margherita Attendolo who had defended a castle, wearing helmet and breast-plate, while her brother Sforza, the renowned soldier of fortune, lay captive in a Neapolitan dungeon. She had heard that story from an eye-witness, not from some old French romance. Could she not hold San Stefano, some day, just as successfully?

Her father knew nothing of her daydreams, but he unconsciously encouraged them by treating her almost like a son. She trotted round stables and kennels at his heels, rode out with him, had her own small crossbow, scrambled up crags, splashed through ice-cold torrents. In San Stefano there was no one to raise shocked eyebrows if his lordship's only child came home looking like a bedraggled beggar.

Finally her mother had rebelled. That took courage, because she was in a weak position and seldom crossed her husband. But for once she had spoken out.

"Do you want our daughter to grow up into a *virago*?"

It was the first time Caterina had heard the word. It seemed to signify a mannish woman. The sort of woman real men did not like.

"If it is God's will that you have no son," her mother continued, "you will have to make do with a son-in-law."

"It seems so," her father agreed sourly. "If we can find one of the right type, some one who can take over San Stefano in the fullness of time –"

"And what family will want to match their boy with an uncouth little ragamuffin? Come to that, who will ever see her if she never moves out of San Stefano? This place is dead. Nobody comes from one year's end to the next."

There had been many discussions after that. Caterina had caught scraps of the talk from time to time.

Half-heartedly, her father had volunteered to open up his neglected town-house in Urbino. But he was a stay-at-home man, absorbed in country sports and the management of his estates, and he seemed relieved when his wife declined. "Even Urbino is only a small city," she pointed out. "There is not much society there. Not that the poor child is really ready for society –"

"Then what the devil –" Father had shown signs of impatience. "Damn it, woman, what *do* you want me to do with her?"

"Well . . . there is this school of the Marquis of Mantua's."

"Where Montefeltro's son is?"

"Federigo? Yes. But there are girls there, I believe. If the Marquis would accept Caterina, they would make a lady of her. She would acquire the polish she cannot get here. She would grow up with her social equals. Boys as well as girls," Caterina's mother added with heavy emphasis, which was not lost on Caterina, straining her ears in a shadowy corner of the room.

So it had been decided. The idea of "social equals" had appealed to Piero Spinelli, whose family pride was out of all proportion to the dilapidated castle and poverty-stricken uplands of which he was lord. He had been delighted too that he would not have to leave home himself for any long period and lodge expensively, bored to distraction, in some distant city merely for the benefit of his daughter's education. Mantua was a splendid idea, even if it was originally his wife's. About Vittorino da Feltre he knew nothing, but apparently the fellow was well spoken of, and, if he was good enough for the Gonzagas of Mantua, he was good enough for the Spinellis. That Caterina would learn Latin and Greek, mathematics and logic, history and literature, as well as ladylike behaviour, was an incidental fact that scarcely registered in his mind.

He had brought her to Mantua and left her here. After a few days the eyes that had at first been sultry with rebellion had grown bright with the wonder of the world.

Now, after a year, she looked back with an indulgent sense of superiority to what seemed the quaint illusions of remote childhood. One could not go against Nature. The old Roman poet, Horace, had said the last word on that: *Though you drive out Nature with a pitchfork, she will still find her way back*. A girl might prefer a wild gallop on the hills to a finicky fiddling with embroidery needles, but in the long run she would have to come to terms with the unalterable limitations of her sex. Caterina knew that she was not cut out to be a *virago*. She was a girl, and at Mantua that seemed much less of a disadvantage. Soon she would be a woman. That too, since her coming here, was a more attractive prospect than once it had been.

There were times, of course, like today, when she was both homesick for San Stefano and depressed by the remembrance of problems still to be solved. Anna said you should leave problems to God. Margherita was a great one for tackling them herself, but in this case she was unable to make any helpful suggestions. For the moment there was nothing, absolutely nothing, to be done about the future of San Stefano.

It was better to push dark thoughts away. She turned from the window and flounced back to her friends. "Let's go out." She snatched the *Aeneid* from Anna's protesting hands. "You must know your Virgil by now. Father sent me some money yesterday; I want to buy a belt. You can both help me to choose."

"We'll ask Federigo to escort us, then," said Margherita. "I know the best shop for belts. Vettori's, just off the market-place."

CHAPTER FIVE

A Very Small Dagger

THEY could go shopping because Vittorino had given his pupils a half-holiday. For that same reason Sandro was lending his father a hand in the shop, unpacking a bale of expensive brocades from Lucca. It was a quiet hour and the place was empty of customers and other staff alike. Then suddenly the street outside came to life with chatter, and the doorway darkened with silhouettes against the afternoon glare.

Vettori went forward. Sandro dropped back into the gloom as he recognised the three girls and Federigo looming behind. Two more boys followed. He was surprised to see that one of them was Taddeo, swaggering in those absurd bag sleeves of his, more like sacks really . . . his outline was quite unmistakable. How he fancied himself! What was he doing in this party? He was no friend of Federigo's. Margherita Gonzaga could choose any boy she liked to escort her through the town: surely she wouldn't pick Taddeo? The unwelcome thought occurred to Sandro that Caterina might have asked him . . . No, he couldn't believe that an intelligent girl like Caterina would have any use for the lout. He decided that Taddeo, being noted for his thick skin, must have inflicted himself on the party uninvited.

The girls were asking to see belts. His father displayed

33

them in the doorway, velvet belts and dyed leather belts, belts with gold or silver studs, belts stitched with tiny pearls. He dangled them in the dusty sunshine. They winked and flashed and twitched like living snakes. The girls fingered, admired, commented, argued. The boys, tiring of the transaction, wandered separately through the shop, examining goods of more interest to them.

There was something for every one in the Vettori shop. Boys who were bored with gossamer veils and painted wedding-chests, silver plate and church vestments, could turn to spurs, saddles and masculine gear of every kind. Breastplates glimmered, a great fan of swords splayed glittering across one wall, faceless helmets looked blankly down from their wooden pegs. There were gauntlets, daggers, leg-pieces, spare studs, buckles. Coats of mail hung from a rack, their close-knit metal rings rippling at a prod of the finger.

"There's money in arms," Sandro's father often said. "Someone's always fighting somebody else." And the whole system of war, he had explained, favoured the arms dealer. There were so many different states in Italy, and so small, most of them, that they could not afford to keep permanent armies of their own. They hired soldiers of fortune, condottieri, captains who in turn hired rank-and-file troopers at so much per head, so many men for six months, say, or a year. When these troopers were out of work, they often had to sell their arms and be fitted out again when they signed a fresh contract. This meant a constant turnover of stock, and a good business-man picked up his profit every time, buying cheap when peace brought unemployment to the soldiers, selling dear when war broke out and every one clamoured for arms. There were bargains after every victory: the losers ran for safety and sold their equipment for anything they

34

could get, while the winners had all the surplus to dispose of that they had collected from the battlefield. That was when the wise merchant filled his warehouse at rock-bottom prices. He could be certain of clearing his stock next year, for the losers always wanted their revenge and started another campaign.

"There's only one man who never loses," Sandro's father would say with a knowing chuckle, "and he's not a soldier." He did not mind how far away the wars were fought. There were Vettori agents in Milan, Bologna and several other cities. "If you've a nose for a profitable deal," he told Sandro, "you can smell it halfway across Italy."

Sandro was uncomfortable when his father talked like that. To him it seemed an unattractive smell. His own nose was happier in a book. He would never make a businessman.

Even now, catching fragments of the conversation, he squirmed at his father's tone, so smooth, so deferential, as he steered Caterina towards a more expensive belt. Caterina was only a girl, Sandro's equal in school, but here she was a customer to be fussed over – especially since the Marquis's own daughter was with her and a liveried servant in the street outside.

"A special price to you, young lady . . ."

Sandro prayed that his father would not suddenly call him forward to bring out more stock. Trapped in his corner behind the bales of cloth, he could not reach the staircase or the back door to the yard without being noticed.

Taddeo had come nearest to him, but luckily Taddeo was intent on examining a dagger in a red velvet sheath. He balanced it in his hand, slid the blade in and out, almost lovingly. He seemed unable to put it down.

Sandro knew that dagger. It was the smallest he had ever seen. But he knew that it was no toy. Only yesterday the Marquis had been explaining that you did not need a long sword to kill your enemy. A mere finger-length of steel would go deep enough if you knew where to strike, but of course the whole art of the armourer was designed to stop you. Daggers were really for emergencies, when men were not dressed for battle.

Taddeo was clearly fascinated by the miniature weapon. If it had been any one else, Sandro would have stepped forward, named the price and made an easy sale, which would have delighted his father and shown that his studious son was not completely without enterprise. But nothing would have induced him to play shopboy to Taddeo.

Still holding the dagger, Taddeo turned his eyes to the group in the doorway, to Federigo, whose back was turned as he examined a painting, and to the other boy, who was fingering a pair of stirrups. Sandro ducked behind the bales just in time as the Perugian youth glanced in his direction.

"I shall have the blue one!" Caterina announced happily as though the whole world had been waiting breathlessly for her decision. Every one gathered round to admire her purchase. Coins clinked. Sandro's father murmured compliments. In another moment they would all have gone and Sandro would have escaped embarrassment.

Instead, without pausing to consider the consequences, he found himself running forward and catching Taddeo by his silly sleeve.

"Taddeo!"

The bigger boy spun round, startled, then looked relieved when he saw who it was.

"Where did *you* spring from? What do you want?"

"That dagger."

"What dagger?"

"The little dagger, the one you were holding just now."

The whole party turned to see what was the matter. Sandro's father asked anxiously, "Some trouble?"

"Your son," said Taddeo grandly, "seems to think I have stolen a dagger."

Everyone exclaimed at once. "Sandro!" His father sounded incredulous. "Oh, what a thing to say!" Anna bleated piously. "Oh, I think that's wicked!"

"I saw him with it! Where is it now, then?" Sandro pointed desperately to the empty place on the counter. His father at least knew that the dagger had been there. But to his consternation his father seemed concerned only with flustered apologies to Taddeo.

"I am sure there is some mistake . . . What were you thinking of, Sandro — even to suggest such a thing — a young gentleman like this —" He turned back to the indignant Taddeo. "We ask your pardon, sir. We hope you will allow the incident —"

"One moment, Master Vettori," Federigo interrupted politely. "Your son is not a fool. And he is not a liar. He must have had some reason. Sandro, on your honour, did you *see* Taddo take this dagger?"

Sandro wished by now that he had never opened his mouth. "Not *take* it," he admitted miserably. "But he was holding it — and he seemed to look all round to make sure that nobody was watching —"

"You little devil!" cried Taddeo.

"But that's a terrible thing to say about any one," Anna was wailing. Sandro's father was choking with rage.

"And it's not there now!" Sandro concluded defiantly.

Federigo was the calmest of them all, but his eyes were troubled. "You can't swear that he took it?"

"No."

"I'm afraid it isn't good enough, Sandro. You really mustn't accuse people of things like that if you can't prove them."

"Do *you* think I'm a liar?" Sandro felt the scalding tears well into his eyes.

Federigo hesitated for an instant. "No," he said gently. As Taddeo exploded with righteous fury Federigo swung round to explain. "I'm not suggesting anything, Taddeo – except that young Sandro must have made an honest mistake. It is rather dark over there." It was extraordinary how Federigo had taken charge of the situation. Even Sandro's father deferred to him. "As Taddeo denies it, I don't see what else you can do, Sandro, but admit you were mistaken."

"I'm sure –" Sandro began. Then, at a scowl from his father, he fell silent. What was the use of feeling sure if you couldn't prove anything? He would have liked to run his fingers over Taddeo's quilted doublet and those immense sleeves. But if Taddeo would not volunteer to be searched, it would be an unforgivable insult to suggest it. He must get out of this appalling situation as best he could. He felt the girls' eyes boring into him. He dared not imagine what they were all thinking. "I'm sorry," he forced himself to say. "If I have made a mistake, I – I apologise."

Somehow the wretched scene was brought to a close. Master Vettori soothed Taddeo's dented dignity, even gave him (and this for Sandro was the crowning irony) a ring to help him forget the unpleasantness. The young people filed out, and Sandro's father whipped round upon him, dropping his mask of glib politeness.

"Imbecile!"

"I'm sorry, Father, but I still think —"

"You don't think about the effect on my business. Suppose he complains to the Marquis? Or the Lady Margherita mentions it?"

"I was only trying to save your stock," Sandro pointed out in self-defence. He stooped to check that the dagger had not fallen unnoticed to the floor. "You can see for yourself, it's not here. If he *didn't* take it —"

"Of course he took it!"

"Then —" Sandro's jaw dropped.

"A trader learns to balance his losses," said his father irritably. "You don't fuss over a single item if it means offending important customers. This could cost me a thousand times as much in lost business. Really, boy, you should be old enough to understand these things. I don't know what I'm going to do with you. Especially if I'm now told that the Marquis won't have you in his school after this!"

The possibility had not occurred to Sandro. He was speechless, and the appalling thought weighed on his mind for the rest of that most unhappy half-holiday. He was full of forebodings when he returned to the Castello at supper-time, wondering whether its gates would be closed against him for ever after tonight.

It was not often that boys were sent away from the school. As it happened there was an expulsion that evening, though apparently it had nothing to do with what had taken place in the shop.

As the boys rose from the supper-tables, heard grace, and dispersed for their usual free hour of recreation, Master Vittorino was seen to beckon Taddeo. For once there was no hint of a smile on the old scholar's lips. "I am afraid that our talk can be postponed no longer," he said. Taddeo followed him to his study, the door closed behind them, and no one ever knew exactly what words passed during the next half-hour.

Taddeo did not come into lessons on the morning after that, nor did he appear again in the school. There was guesswork about the reason, but nobody could be certain.

Master Vittorino was late for his first class. While the pupils waited, Caterina leant forward on her bench and Sandro felt her breath warm against his ear.

"You know that Taddeo has gone?"

"They say so," he whispered back. It was the first time she had ever spoken to him.

"It had nothing to do with yesterday." Trust the girls, he thought to himself amusedly, to have ferreted out the truth while the boys speculated wildly. But Caterina had advantages, being Margherita Gonzaga's friend.

"Master Vittorino sees through people who aren't genuine," she went on confidently. "He's had his eye on Taddeo. He was never right for this place."

"No?"

"He didn't really care about learning. He was using the school – to get to know what he calls 'the right people'. Remember, his family were thrown out of Perugia. He has to make his own way in the world. Master Vittorino gave him every chance, but he was bad for the school. One rotten apple spoils the whole barrel."

"It seems a bit hard on Taddeo –"

"Rubbish! If you weren't new here," said Caterina darkly, and paused, her silence hinting at nameless iniquities. Then she went on, "Taddeo will always look after Taddeo. He'll do well enough."

Just then Master Vittorino bustled in, apologising for his lateness just as if they were men and women as old as himself. It was time to go through the Virgil they had prepared. But one pleasant thought hovered in Sandro's mind throughout the lesson, coming between him and the adventures of Aeneas: all yesterday's fears had been unfounded, and he was never going to see Taddeo again.

In assuming this, however, he was over-optimistic.

CHAPTER SIX

The Forbidden Book

A YEAR had passed. They were on Horace's *Odes* now.
Caterina studied the lines she would have to recite tomorrow.

Alas, Postumus, Postumus, the fleeting years slip by.

Curious, she reflected, how obsessed older people were
with this business of passing Time! They were always on
about it in their poems.

To her it seemed an age since she had ridden down the
winding road from San Stefano, yet in fact it was only
fourteen months. Time seemed longer when it was packed
so full of new experiences, ideas, relationships.

Now the seasons were coming round again. For the
second autumn she would miss the flame and russet and
gold of the steeply hung woodlands, the mists, the rumble
of unseen waterfalls hurtling down . . . and then the
winter silvering of the stark uplands . . . and after that
the sudden starring of the pastures with the little flowers
of spring. In Mantua the seasons meant quite different
things. Winter spelt fog, dank and draughty arcades, and
a waste of leaden grey flood water lapping the embank-
ments. Summer brought stench, mosquitoes and fever.

Of course, there were compensations. Here there was
always something happening – carnivals, balls, church
ceremonies, pageants, parades, horse-races. There were

days when life seemed one blaze of torchlight, shiver of trumpets, clang of bells — when one's pulse thrilled to the incessant rhythm of the marching drums. San Stefano was a tomb compared with Mantua. Yes, there were many compensations. And foremost among them she was beginning to list, in her secret heart, Federigo Montefeltro.

Everyone in the school liked Federigo. One could say that without exaggeration, now that the unlamented Taddeo Tregani had departed. This liking took different forms, from the gruff approval of the Marquis to the hero-worship of the smaller boys and the moonstruck admiration of the girls, for one of Federigo's likeable characteristics was his willingness to help the juniors, whether with lessons or sport.

Sandro was never one of the hero-worshippers but he looked up to Federigo as a natural leader. He was not going to push himself forward, as some did, and try to curry favour — not that Federigo gave much encouragement to that sort of thing — but a word of praise from the older boy gave him a specially warm feeling inside. A word of praise — or a communicated enthusiasm. Sandro's one weakness was mathematics. Words he loved, numbers baffled him. "I can't see the use of all this," he groaned one day.

"Can't you?" Federigo sounded surprised. "But mathematics are the cornerstone of learning!"

He began to talk enthusiastically about architecture. How, if you didn't learn mathematics, could you build a palace, get the room proportions right, the courtyards symmetrical, the windows, pillars, everything, as they must be? How could you work out the cost, calculate the thousands of bricks, tons of stone, areas to be floored with tiles or marble?

43

Sandro laughed. "Are you thinking of building a palace?"

"No — but how I'd like to. Just think, a palace as splendid as this one, but all your own ideas! And not stuck down here, with mud and mosquitoes, but up in the hills, where you could see for miles —"

"A castle in the air!"

"You're right. That's all it will be, so far as I'm concerned. Still," Federigo went on philosophically, "I expect I'll find mathematics useful in other ways. You need it for fortifications and gunnery."

Every one knew that Federigo was going to be a soldier. What else was there for him to do? A count's son could hardly become an architect or an artist, still less a merchant. The only alternative for a gentleman was to become a priest and end his days as a bishop or, with luck, a cardinal. But that meant not marrying, and it was hard to picture the lively Federigo following such a vocation. A profession he must have, however, for Urbino would be inherited by his young half-brother, the Count's legal heir. Federigo would have to do as many another penniless gentleman had done before him — become a condottiere, raise his personal army, and serve whatever government would employ him: the Duke of Milan, the Florentine Republic, or the Pope in Rome.

Would he make a successful condottiere? Sandro wondered. According to Master Vettori, such mercenary generals were no better than hired cut-throats, for ever changing sides, taking bribes and plundering honest people, friend and foe indiscriminately. That didn't sound like Federigo. Would his even temper fit him for such a ferocious role?

When the next tournament was held in the piazza, Sandro's doubts vanished. Federigo and the other older boys were allowed to compete in special events. There was jousting with light lances and fencing with blunt swords, involving no danger beyond a few tumbles and bruises. That afternoon, though, Sandro saw a transformed Federigo, fighting like a demon. He shone in the individual contests, he captained the side which won the mock battle. Every one applauded wildly when he went up to receive his prize from Margherita's elder sister.

That Sunday afternoon Federigo overwhelmed more than his opponents in the lists. From the damask-hung dais Caterina watched in a frenzy, agonised when he looked like being unhorsed, ecstatic when again and again he triumphed. He was so fearless a rider, so dynamic a leader, so modest a victor. By the end of the tournament she had no doubt left: she was in love.

Of course, she vowed, it must remain a secret; no one must guess. That night she lay awake for hours, going over the day's excitements. Love-sick maidens, according to all the romances, were supposed to toss and turn, bedewing their pillows with vain tears. She could do none of these things, for fear of waking Margherita and Anna, who shared the great bed with her. But she lay rigid, staring up into the darkness. In the morning Anna made tactless remarks about the rings under her eyes, and even the kindly Master Vittorino criticised her slipshod Greek translation. She was well aware that her jaded brain was not functioning properly.

So far as Margherita was concerned, the secret survived only until bedtime came again. As usual the Marquis's daughter was brisk and encouraging.

"It's nothing to be ashamed of. All the girls fall in love with Federigo."

"_I_ haven't," protested Anna, overhearing.

"Oh, well, you don't —" Margherita paused and

hurriedly rephrased her retort. "I mean, I'm not counting you."

Caterina sprawled wearily on the bed. "If every one falls in love with him, what chance have *I* got?"

"Better than most! With your complexion – and that chestnut hair," said Margherita loyally. "And I'm sure you're *going* to have a good figure –"

"No, the whole idea's silly. It's hopeless. I don't want to talk about it."

But of course she did want to, and they discussed the subject in all its aspects long after they should have been asleep.

"I wish you wouldn't go on saying you've no chance," said Margherita at last. "There's a simple way to test that."

"How?"

"Find out what the stars say."

"But –"

"Leave it all to me." Margherita was not a Gonzaga for nothing. Management was in her blood. "I'll talk to my father's astrologer and get him to cast your horoscope." She silenced Caterina's protest. "I shan't tell him whose it is. I'll need your date of birth and hour of birth – the year's the same as mine, of course, 1425 –"

"I don't know the time," said Caterina weakening, "but I've heard Father say that I gave my first cry just as the sun came over the horizon."

"Marvellous! *He* can work out the time from his astrological almanacs. He'll do anything for me," said Margherita confidently. "This is the best way to clear up any doubts."

"But surely he can't tell me for certain –"

"No, but you'll get an indication. I mean, if your horoscope shows that you're going to marry a foreigner, or

46

you're destined to die young, or end your days as a virgin, then there'll be no point in worrying any further."

"Thank you very much," said Caterina tartly.

Five days later the three girls were poring intently over an impressive-looking paper covered with the astrologer's spidery black handwriting. Most of the horoscope was couched in a puzzling jargon: such and such a star had been in the ascendant in this particular "house" of the heavens, and the "aspect" of this planet to that had been "sesqui-quadrate" (whatever *that* might mean) whereas another pair of planets had been in "conjunction". Only towards the end of the document did it become clear and interesting.

"*The indications are,*" read Margherita, "*that the subject will marry happily and be blessed with child-ren –*"

"I expect he always says that," said Anna, depressingly. She rather disapproved of the whole inquiry.

"He wouldn't say anything that wasn't in the horoscope. Don't be a jealous little cat. Now, where was I? *And that she will find a husband among those with whom she has been acquaintd in childhood.* What about that?" Margherita demanded triumphantly.

Caterina wavered. Hope sprang within her, but commonsense forced her to say, "It could be any of the boys here. Or someone at San Stefano."

"True," Margherita admitted. The horoscope offered no more definite information. "What we really want is Federigo's horoscope as well, to see if it points in the same way. Like geometry."

Caterina could not see how geometry connected with her future love-life. Her friend explained impatiently. "If his said that *he* would marry someone he'd known as a boy, it would be a strong indication like two lines intersecting. We must find out when Federigo was born, bring up the subject ever so casually –"

"Margherita! We couldn't possibly. You're forgetting."

Reluctantly Margherita admitted that it might be too embarrassing. Federigo himself was probably vague about the time of his birth. When children were born in palaces such details were recorded. When they arrived illegitimately, the event was not given the same enthusiastic publicity.

"We shall have to do without *his* horoscope," conceded Margherita, "and yours alone doesn't carry us much further. Never mind. We'll think of something else."

The "something else", which Margherita suggested a few days later, was a love-potion. Caterina would have to find a suitable opportunity and slip it into Federigo's drink. This seemed to Margherita a better idea than the horoscope, for it meant really doing something to influence events.

"But where could I get a love-potion?" said Caterina dubiously. "And how do we know they work?"

"I don't know whether they work, but I've always wanted to try."

"Isn't it witchcraft?" Anna inquired. "Do you think that Christians ought –"

"Are you calling *my grandmother* a witch?"

"Oh, *no*, Margherita, of course not!"

"Well, my mother has a book which *her* mother kept. She put recipes in it and curses and all sorts of things. Mother's forbidden us to look at it, she has it in her room under lock and key, but I know where the key is –"

"You wouldn't be so wicked!" said Anna.

"Not for my own sake. But in the name of friendship," said Margherita nobly. "I'm quite certain there's a formula in it for a love-potion."

"Well, you're not to," Caterina insisted. "Not on my account."

"But we must do *something*. We can't have you mooning about for ever."

"I am not mooning. I – I wish I'd never told you anything."

"Do you think we shouldn't have guessed, dear girl? I mean, the way you look at him!"

But Caterina stood on her dignity. She would conceal her feelings. She would not resort to tricks to rouse Federigo's interest.

Somehow she kept to her resolution for another week. It was a miserable, humiliating time. She lurked in Federigo's path, manoeuvred what looked like accidental encounters, contrived tiny services to render him. Federigo always had a smile and a pleasant word for her, but then he had that for every one. Blast his unfailing courtesy, she said to herself bitterly. It would be better if he were rude. At least it would mean that he was singling her out from all the others.

How long she could have borne it she never knew, for this phase ended abruptly with shattering news, brought fresh by Margherita from her father's dinner-table. Federigo's time as a hostage was over. A dispatch had arrived for the Marquis from the Most Serene Republic of Venice. The Count of Urbino's son was to be sent home with appropriate escort and safe-conduct.

"So you see," said Margherita dramatically, "we must act at once."

"How do you mean?" Caterina looked as hopeless as she felt.

"Don't say you've forgotten! Grandmother's book! I

shall sneak it up to our room tonight, while Mother is at supper."

"But I told you—"

"It's your last chance," Margherita assured her grimly. "He's going home next week."

Caterina let herself be overruled. Margherita was right, it was now or never. If this incomparable young man was not to pass out of her life, some drastic action was necessary. She was prepared to try anything.

That night the three girls huddled over the forbidden volume, their heads casting jerky shadows on its musty pages. There was a good deal of nervous giggling. Anna was as bad as the others, though her feelings were divided between fascination and disapproval.

Margherita's grandmother had certainly bequeathed an extraordinary collection of feminine secrets, amassed during a long, eventful and not entirely blameless life.

There were beauty hints. *"To keep the hands soft and white take some mustard, mixed with apple and bitter almonds, rub it into your hands at bedtime, and sleep in tight leather gloves . . ."* Laurel leaves and pine-resin, added to the water on wash-day, made the linen fragrant. A girl should study the ways to display her best features without seeming immodest: indoors, she might show just a little leg, provided her stockings were clean and her slippers elegant, but in the country she could make opportunities to reveal rather more, for instance by jumping over small streams and ditches.

These assorted hints were jumbled with cookery recipes, rules of etiquette, and remedies for sickness, written into the book just as Margherita's grandmother had picked them up. One never knew what was coming next, but it was all so absorbing that they could have sat up all night.

"There's a horrible ointment here called *Oil of a Red-haired Dog!*"

"Oh, look, it says that if you wear a piece of coral it's a protection against being poisoned!"

"Anna, it tells you how to get rid of spots," said Caterina tactlessly.

"And unwanted babies!" said Margherita, raptly studying the page opposite.

"Oh, I think it's *wicked*," said Anna, but she read every word.

It took them a long time to find a love-potion. At last Margherita let out a cry of triumph. "Here you are!"

"*A Potent Purge for them that be Costive —*" read Anna dubiously.

"No, stupid! The next one. *A Sovereign Remedy for Unrequited Love.*"

"Ooh!"

As they bent closer over it in the candle-light, they were startled by a distant bell. "Holy Heaven," said Margherita, "it's late! I must get this book back in Mother's room. We'll have to copy this out. Anna, *you* always have your pen and ink. Quick, girl."

Obediently, if a shade sulkily, Anna produced quill, ink-bottle, and a piece of paper, and wrote down the ingredients as Margherita dictated them. Caterina let them get on with it. She only half believed in the idea. Part of her wanted it to work. At the same time her pride rebelled. She would prefer Federigo to love her for what she really was, not because of some magical concoction poured into his drink.

There seemed to be a lot of ingredients, but, as Margherita exclaimed, nothing grisly or revolting or difficult to obtain. No monkey's blood, dried toad, or crushed scorpion. They could find everything in the store-cupboards, the herb garden, or the fields outside. "*And finally*," ran the prescription, "*let the lover's own name be writ on a paper, and this paper be placed in the liquor until the ink dissolves therein.*"

"That's all," said Margherita. "Have you got it, Anna? Oh, you *are* slow!"

"I can't write any faster. Just let me check with the book, Margherita."

"Very well. But be quick, do! If Mother catches me –"

"All right, there you are." There was almost as much snap in Anna's tone as in the way she closed the volume and thrust it into Margherita's impatient clutches. Margherita fled downstairs. Anna picked up her quill and inserted a word or two. "I *had* missed one of the ingredients," she explained. "Margherita bustles me so."

"Well, thank you very much," said Caterina awkwardly.

Once the wild flowers and herbs were collected, there was no difficulty about preparing the mixture. The Marchioness believed that all girls, however exalted their rank, should know something of cookery, household management and nursing. So, while the boys were busy outside with their wrestling and fencing, they had the run of the palace kitchens, the still-rooms and store-rooms. With her two friends to help and screen the exact nature of her activities, Caterina was able to get all the items together, simmer them for the stipulated time, and transfer the resulting liquor to a small flask, which she carried unnoticed to her room. There, with bumping heart and shaky fingers, she wrote *Caterina Spinelli* on a narrow slip of paper and pushed it down the neck of the flask.

How to get the stuff into Federigo's drink?

The resourceful Margherita had her answer to that difficulty. At her suggestion, backed by her elder sister,

Federigo's last day was to be marked by a picnic on the opposite bank of the Lower Lake. At a picnic, she pointed out to Caterina, they would all mingle informally, and any girl with an ounce of enterprise could approach the boy she fancied and slip something into his cup.

Everything went according to plan. The weather was perfect. Just sufficient breeze ruffled the water to refresh the summer air. They rowed across in a flotilla of small boats, with servants and stacks of delicious provisions, singing to the accompaniment of a lute. Looking back at the long russet walls and towers of the Castello, and their reflection hung upside down in the lake, Caterina realised with a pang that Mantua had its own dreamy beauty, though so different from that of her native hills, to which fortunate Federigo was returning tomorrow. That thought gave her a much keener pang and reminded her of the business in hand.

It was, as Margherita had promised, absurdly easy.

After some dancing and games on the grassy bank, they all sprawled in the shade of the cypresses and enjoyed the cold meats, the cakes, the slices of melon, the amusing little saffron-tinted jellies in the shape of animals, and the other delicacies the servants had unpacked. There was much laughter and larking, much impulsive running from group to group, much handing of dishes and refilling of cups with watered wine. So, quite naturally, Federigo found himself face to face with Caterina and accepting the cup she held out to him.

She raised her own cup. "Your health, Federigo! A safe journey to Urbino!"

He smiled down at her, and her heart turned over inside her. "Thank you. Here's to you, too, Caterina — and no doubt we shall meet again someday, perhaps in Urbino." He drained his cup with a gallant flourish. She caught a startled look in his eyes. Wiping his lips, he gasped, "That was strong."

"Watered wine is for boys," she said, and turned away to hide her confusion.

The next morning, every one gathered in the courtyard to see Federigo ride away with his little cavalcade. The three girls were almost beside themselves. "You'll see an immediate change in him," said Margherita. "Of course, he'll have to go home, it's all arranged, but he'll make sure that he sees you again very soon. I wonder what he'll say to you. Perhaps he'll just *look*, and it'll be written all over his face."

When they saw Federigo they were struck by his pallor. He exhibited every sign of having passed a disturbed night. When, as he made his farewells, he came to Caterina he certainly regarded her with a distinctly curious expression, which she could not interpret as one of passion. And, for all his invariable good manners, his demeanour towards her was tepid.

When he had gone, Caterina muttered between sobs, "It didn't work."

"I think it did," said Anna in a strangely satisfied voice.

"It may take time," said Margherita optimistically, "or perhaps he was struggling to hide new feelings he doesn't yet fully understand. It must have been a shock to his system, a drink like that."

"Must have," said Anna.

CHAPTER SEVEN

"In the Name of God and of Profit"

IF Caterina Spinelli was growing up fast and becoming aware of new moods and emotions, Sandro Vettori, too, was beginning to realise how much he had changed since starting at the school. Thinking back to those early days, to his first glimpse of Caterina galloping along the margin of the lagoon, and the months thereafter when he had sat on the bench in front of her in class, he found it hard to believe that he had been so little affected.

Of course, he told himself loftily, they had both been so *young* then, himself a shy, studious little boy, and Caterina a flat-chested child. Now, with Federigo and many of the other seniors gone, they would soon be among Master Vittorino's elder pupils. Already Sandro was enjoying the new sensation of authority.

"What on earth do *you* think you're doing?" he demanded good-humouredly, interrupting a riotous group of juniors during the free hour before bedtime.

"Playing at Plato!" gasped the only boy who was not speechless with laughter.

"Playing at Plato?" Sandro raised his eyebrows in kindly puzzlement. Unconsciously he had modelled himself on Federigo.

"Watch, Sandro!"

They resumed their absurd, delirious antics. They

55

staggered round the hall in couples, back to back, arms tightly linked. They tried to run races, which was difficult, since either they had to go sideways like crabs or one boy of each pair had to go backwards in step with his partner.

"What has this to do with Plato?" asked Sandro when they had all collapsed in a breathless heap.

"*The Symposium!* We're reading it with Master Vittorino!"

Light began to dawn. The next day, he was curious enough to go back to the relevant passage in *The Symposium*. When he had read it, over a year ago, he had made no more of it than these juniors, who had turned it into a noisy game.

"*The sexes were not always two as they are now,*" Plato had written, more than eighteen hundred years before, putting his fanciful theory into the mouth of Aristophanes. "*Primitive man was round, his back and sides forming a circle. He had four hands and four feet, one head with two faces, turned opposite ways, four ears, two sexual organs, and everything else correspondingly. He could walk upright as men walk nowadays, backwards or forwards to taste, but he could also roll over and over at great speed, turning on his four hands and his four feet, like a tumbler . . .*"

It wasn't surprising, thought Sandro with a smile, that the small boys had found this notion irresistibly funny. He read on, more interested in the serious idea which Plato had embodied in his fantasy.

The gods of Olympus had grown tired of men's insolence and discussed whether or not to wipe them out with thunderbolts. Zeus had decided on a compromise. To reduce each man's strength and pride, he would split him in half down the middle, like an apple, leaving him with only two arms and two legs. And so, explained Plato, "*each of us is always looking for his other half. And when he encounters that half, the missing complement of himself, the two of them are lost in a daze of love and friendship, and do not want to be out of each other's sight, even for an instant. Such are the people who spend all their lives together — yet they could not explain what they seek from each other.*" It was the very expression of Man's ancient need. "*Human nature,*" Plato concluded, "*was originally one, and we were a whole, and the desire and pursuit of the whole is called Love.*"

Was there anything in this ancient philosopher's fable? At least, thought Sandro, it explained his own strange new yearning to be close to Caterina on every possible occasion, to talk to her and win her approval. Could she possibly be, in Plato's sense, his missing half? He had to admit to himself, sadly, that she showed no signs of a similar attraction to him, as the theory seemed to require.

Far otherwise. According to what some of the boys had whispered several months ago, she cherished a passion for Federigo da Montefeltro. Much chance Sandro would have against the Count of Urbino's debonair son!

A little while afterwards news reached Mantua which gave him a slender hope. "Have you heard?" Anna was gleefully whispering to Caterina on the back bench. "Federigo is married! To a girl named Gentile Brancaleone."

Caterina sounded interested, but not at all upset. "Really? But I'm not surprised he's got married. He'll be sixteen next birthday." Her voice suggested that Federigo belonged to another, older generation.

Anna was clearly disappointed. "Don't you care? I thought you were madly in love with him."

"I thought so too – ages ago. One has these childish infatuations, but one soon gets over them."

So, thought Sandro, listening with both ears, the field was still open. But it needed a great deal of optimism to believe that he and Caterina, even if they were Platonic halves, would ever be allowed to come together.

Any hope he might have clung to soon shrank to vanishing point. Caterina was going home, back to that remote little town in the valleys of the Marches, where he would never see her again and where in any case, no doubt, her parents would soon be finding her a suitable husband.

The news plunged him into gloom. When, on the Sunday following, his father informed him that his own schooldays were numbered and he must shortly enter the family business, this second blow could hardly increase his misery.

"I need you," said his father. "I'm sending Francesco to Genoa, to get experience with our agent there. And I can't do without some member of the family to help me in the shop. There's been too much pilfering. I haven't eyes in the back of my head."

The pilfering, it appeared, had not been done by customers. It was the work of an apprentice, who had been stealthily robbing the stock for the past six months, and had now made off, only God knew where. What infuriated Vettori was that this youth had been the trusted one, who slept on a rickety trestle-bed at the back of the shop to guard it during the night. This bed Sandro took over, with a hand-bell beside him to sound the alarm if he was awakened by suspicious noises.

It was very different, he reflected ruefully as he made up his bed on the first evening after the street-door was bolted and the window shuttered, very different indeed from those sociable bed-times at school when the other boys had crowded round to listen to his stories. Not that he much minded being put down here alone, away from the rest of the family. He was not truly one of them. Mistress Vettori never let him forget that. He was happier with his own thoughts in the warm, rather stuffy darkness, with the dry smells of cloth, leather and pine-wood shelves.

How different, too, were the day-times, after the lessons and discussions with Master Vittorino, the blissful hours of reading, the riding and swimming, the strenuous games, the singing and dancing! The books that concerned him now were his father's heavy ledgers, each of them solemnly inscribed on its first page, *In the Name of God and of Profit*. Instead of the mathematics which Federigo had helped him to grasp, there was now only the simple arithmetic of scales and yard-stick. To reckon up accounts, his father insisted on his using the squared board and bowls of little counters, variously coloured – like a child's game, thought Sandro rebelliously, when even he could have worked out the right answer on a scrap of paper or even in his head.

Then there were the letters to read and answer – dull business correspondence, sometimes hardly literate, not at all like the elegant letters of Cicero and Pliny they had studied at school. Sandro yawned over the lists, the prices, the complaints about delay or bad quality, the excuses. Only once in a while came a flash of interest – a reference to piracy or shipwreck, to the capture of a city or the cutting of a trade-route by some hostile condottiere. The letters might come from far-off places, Paris and London, Barcelona and Bruges, but they brought only the faintest whiff of romance. Mostly they stuck to

the point, and that point – the whole point in life –
seemed to be the making of money.

Once, stung to rebellion, Sandro quoted to his father
the pious phrase heading the first page in the ledger. "In
the name of God and of Profit . . . Why the repetition?"

"Repetition? What do you mean?"

"Profit *is* your God, isn't it?"

"Don't be blasphemous!"

"*I* think it is blasphemous to put God's name in your
account-books."

His father scowled. "I left you too long at that school.
They've made you talk like a preacher."

There were times when Sandro admitted, in his heart,
that he was unfair to his father. The world must have
merchants. Everyone wanted the goods, and those goods
had to be found, carried from country to country, and
distributed. How many books would he have managed
to read, himself, for instance, if it had not been worth
somebody's while to have fresh copies written out and
sold? You could not blame a merchant for being keen.
A soldier fought to win, a schoolboy played a game to
win . . . A businessman would soon go bankrupt if
he did not do the same.

I suppose, he concluded sombrely, it's just that I am
not cut out for this particular game.

His stepmother's attitude did not help. She was pregnant again, inclined to be irritable, and more than ever
jealous of Sandro's presence in the house. Had she not
given her husband enough children to provide for, and
to help in his business, and was she not about to produce
yet another? She was determined that Sandro should
never share equally with her own sons and daughters.
She watched him suspiciously, alert for any pretext to
lever him out of his position.

One evening, when his father was out at a supper-party with some of the other merchants, she came upon him bent over some files of old correspondence.

"You're working late!"

"Yes." He was, in fact, making a conscientious effort to get the hang of this business. During the daytime, what with customers, errands and constant odd jobs, there was no chance to study the complicated transactions involved in some of these deals with distant foreign companies.

"Did your father give you permission to rummage about in these cupboards?"

He winced at the suspicion in her tone. "No –"

"I thought not!"

"But he doesn't expect me to ask permission! I'm allowed to look at any of the files," Sandro protested.

"You wisely choose a moment when his back is turned." Her face, already puffy, was flushed and swollen with hatred. "I know your little game! Don't imagine you can fool me."

"I have no 'little game'."

"Oh, yes, you have!" Her anger was rising to the boil. "You're making a nice little nest for yourself in this business while poor Francesco is away in Genoa. You mean to be your father's righthand man, don't you? Make yourself indispensable, get control of the business someday, do my children out of their rights!" Her voice became strident. It rang through the tall house. "It's all so obvious."

The absurd accusation stung him. He fought to control his tongue. All his childhood he had treated her with the utmost respect. But he felt himself almost a man, now, and there was a limit to the insults a man could be

61

expected to take. He answered with what he hoped was the calm civility Federigo would have shown.

"You are unjust to me, madam. But I make allowances —"

"*Allowances!*" she echoed scornfully.

"Pregnant women have odd fancies —"

She struck him across the cheek.

"You should not upset yourself," he said. "It is bad for you." He stood up, put the files back in the cupboard, and left the room.

I can't stand much more of this, he told himself. He said nothing to his father when, some hours later, he had to rise from his bed in the shop to unbar the door for him. He had not been asleep, he had been lying wide awake, revolving all sorts of desperate plans, but his father's slurred speech and wine-laden breath warned him that it was no time for sensible discussions.

He did not have to broach the matter himself the next morning. Giovanni Vettori drew him aside.

"She's been on to you again?"

"Yes, Father."

"She told me. She spent the rest of the night telling me. God, my head aches! I'm sorry, Sandro, really I am. But I can't curb her tongue. I'm in a difficult position."

"So am I," said Sandro quietly.

"I'll try to make it up to you. I'll find some way. But we must be discreet, she's got this unreasoning jealousy. Still, if she thinks I'm going to turn you out, she's very much —"

"No, Father, please." Sandro checked the bluster, knowing how quickly it would wilt under the woman's nagging. "There'll be no peace in this house while I'm here. She's your wife, I mustn't make trouble between you."

"My dear boy –"

"You've brought me up. I can stand on my own feet now."

"No need for that. Yet . . . you may be right." There was shamefaced relief in his father's eyes, and already those quick wits were adjusting to the situation. "It might be better if you went to one of our branches in another city – I could easily arrange it –"

"That's not what I mean, Father. I've come to the conclusion, I'm not suited to business. Please, you have a consignment of goods starting for Bergamo on Thursday. Will you lend me a horse and let me go with the convoy? So far, that is. I want to branch off to Brescia."

"Brescia?" His father's jaw dropped. "They're making a detour especially to avoid Brescia. There's fighting there. The town's besieged."

"I know. Young Federigo da Montefeltro is there. He's got his first command – they say he has a company of four hundred men, with a commission from the Duke of Milan."

"But *you* don't want to be a soldier!"

"I don't know," Sandro answered truthfully. "But I do know I don't want to be a merchant."

His father made only a half-hearted attempt to dissuade him. He was clutching at the opportunity to get Sandro out of the house without himself feeling guilty about it. "Of course there are all *sorts* of openings," he admitted in a self-justifying tone. "Montefeltro is a useful contact. And you've got your head screwed on the right way. You'll drop into something that suits you; you're not my son for nothing."

He insisted on treating Sandro generously. He would not lend him a horse, he would give him one. And when he rode out with the mule-train at dawn that Thursday,

63

Sandro was very respectably mounted on a black gelding, Naddo, that had cost twenty-five florins. He had another twenty florins in his purse and a letter of credit, stitched inside his doublet, which any of his father's widely-spread agents would cash for a hundred.

Vettori walked with him to the city gate and blessed him solemnly when the moment came to part.

"In the name of God," he said huskily, at once sad and relieved.

"And of Profit?" said Sandro wickedly.

"Go along with you, boy, and don't be blasphemous."

Three days later Sandro was sitting in Federigo's tent outside the walls of Brescia. He had been a little shy about this meeting. Federigo was a young soldier, now, a married man, and had gone a long way since they had been boys at school together two years ago.

He need not have worried. At a glance he saw that it was still the same Federigo, a little more sun-tanned, a shade broader in the shoulders, but with the same free-and-easy manner, the same smiling welcome and shrewd twinkle in the eye.

They had supper alone. Sandro inquired politely after his wife. Gentile was well, said Federigo. She was a good girl, an orphan. Being an only child, she had brought some inherited lands into the marriage. He was grateful to his father for finding him such a satisfactory partner. Federigo spoke coolly, without obvious enthusiasm. He could not have been a very ardent bridegroom, Sandro thought, or he would not have left Gentile after a few months to go soldiering. He had to remind himself that Federigo was still only seventeen, and his military career was uppermost in his mind. "No," said Federigo, "we haven't been blessed with a child so far." Changing the subject, he asked Sandro what he proposed to do. "*You* don't want to be a soldier," he said, unconsciously echoing Vettori's words.

"Don't you think I could be?"

Federigo eyed him up and down. "Oh, you *could* be. You've filled out a lot. And you used to be quite handy with a sword – do you remember how the Marquis used to roar at us?" He chuckled. "But is it in your nature, Sandro?" he went on in a more serious tone. "My men are a rough bunch; they have to be. It's often a matter of kill or be killed. They think just as much about money as the merchants do, what loot they can pick up, what ransom the prisoners will fetch, how much more pay they can get if they desert to the other side."

Sandro returned his gaze steadily. "Is that how *your* mind works? I can't imagine it."

"No. You're right. I couldn't fight just for the pay. But . . ." Federigo hesitated. Sandro helped him out of his embarrassment.

"You can afford to choose. You're somebody – already. And when you're a big condottiere you'll be even freer. It's the rank-and-file who have to do as they're told."

"It's the way things are."

Federigo talked for a little while about his company. It was organised on the usual basis of so many "lances", each "lance" comprising three persons, a seasoned man-at-arms, his squire who was often just as experienced, and a page who held their horses when they dismounted and generally acted as their orderly. Five "lances" formed a post, five posts a *bandiera* or troop. Federigo had also his headquarters staff, including drummers and trumpeters, and a small contingent of crossbowmen.

"You couldn't possibly join a lance," he said decisively, "except as a page – and you'd hardly like that. You're not old enough to be one of the men-at-arms. Anyhow, these men like to pair with a mate they've campaigned with for years."

"I understand. I can see I'd be no use to you. I haven't the training or the experience."

"Wait. In another way you have." Federigo brightened. It seemed there was an amazing amount of paperwork at headquarters. As commander he received a lump sum from the Duke's general and then it was his responsibility to pay the men their agreed rate according to their grades. Then there was back pay, and pay to be advanced to men who had got into debt, and the complicated share-out of ransoms and money realised from the sale of loot. There were letters to be written, contracts drawn up, bills settled. "It would be child's play to a man like your father," said Federigo, "and it wouldn't be too difficult even to you, after what he's taught you. But it's a nightmare to my staff, and if I ever become 'a big condottiere' – as you so flatteringly prophesy – it will be even worse."

It was not the kind of work Sandro had ever pictured himself doing, but he saw that it offered the only way, for the moment, to earn his keep. He accepted gratefully. He could not help reminding Federigo with a smile: "You promised once – when you were a famous general, I'd go on all your campaigns and write the history of your triumphs!"

"And so you shall! If any. But you'll have to start in a humble way, just as I'm doing myself." Federigo stretched out his arm and refilled their glasses. "You were lucky to find me here."

"Lucky?"

"My father wants me back in Urbino. Sigismondo Malatesta is making trouble on our borders. Father's getting a bit past soldiering, himself, and my half-brother's too young, so it's up to me. As soon as Milan can release me, we'll be on the march for San Stefano."

"San Stefano!"

"You seem to have acquired a habit of echoing everything."

"I'm sorry. But isn't that the town – do you remember Caterina Spinelli?"

"I'm not likely to forget her. A rather beautiful girl. But odd."

"I don't know about odd," said Sandro.

CHAPTER EIGHT

The Town on the Crag

"Home!" said her father, pointing, and she loved him for the sudden tenderness in his voice. Over her horse's ears Caterina saw the town outlined against a white scud of cloud.

San Stefano roosted on a limestone pinnacle, jagged as a rotten tooth, standing up from the green valley floor. Soon she could make out the pale track zigzagging up to vanish into the town gateway like a snake flicking into its hole. Left and right of the arch, the well-remembered walls girdled the crag, clinging to its dizzy facets as best they could. Above the battlements peeped roofs, towers and belfries, buff-coloured and terracotta, higgledy-piggledy. Over all, topping the broken fang, brooded the ancient castle which the Spinellis, for all their family pride, could never hope to make habitable again.

It was good to be home at last, to take the smiling salute of the gate-keeper, and wave back to the people as she rode up through the narrow streets to the odd-shaped slanting piazza. There was the convent, there was San Stefano's church, and there, facing down from the upper side of the square, was the "palace" – she must remember always to call it a palace, or she would hurt her father's feelings, though after the magnificence of Mantua it now seemed to her no more than a big house, and shabby at that. Still, what did it matter? She was home, and here was her mother, radiant, with open arms, sweeping down the front steps to embrace her as she slid from the saddle.

The joys of home-coming began to fade after a day or two.

She looked round with fresh, critical eyes. The Palazzo Spinelli was shabby all right. The stone stairs were worn, dipping along their edges like old kitchen knives. The peeling plaster on the walls had disgusting blotches, the paved floors were irregular. At Mantua there had been tiles and marble slabs underfoot, even soft carpets. The walls had been bright with frescoes, the painted ceilings had glittered with stars. Only now did she realise how soft the beds had been, how crisp and fresh the linen.

How could her parents put up with this place, see nothing wrong?

The massive furniture looked as though it had been knocked together by a forester. There was an unspeakable stench from the privies. How could she ever have grumbled at the stagnant water in Mantua? Talking of water, did nobody wash here? Margherita Gonzaga had washed all over, every day, and the other girls had copied her. Here, when she asked for hot water, scented by boiling herbs in it, the maid stared back at her like a dumbfounded cow.

It was good, of course, to be with her father and mother. It had been a long separation, but that kind of thing was part of life and one must brace oneself for it: many a girl of her age was married and, if she went off to some distant home, might have little prospect of ever seeing her parents again. Thank God, there was no talk yet of anything like that.

It was good to meet some of the older servants, to be told how much she had filled out, and how beautiful a young lady she had become — if she could believe a quarter of their compliments. And it was good to renew friendships with the hounds sprawling in the hall, and to explore the stables, greeting horses she remembered and introducing herself to the new ones. But soon she was hungry for the stimulus of real conversation. You could not exchange ideas with dogs and horses, and talking to parents was not much better.

They were glad to have her back, but they were not really interested in where she had been or what she had been doing. Her mother asked a few obvious questions and let the matter drop. Her father never mentioned Mantua. They were incurious. Slowly she came to realise that what they did not already know and understand did not exist for them.

In the first days she had bubbled over with enthusiasm. She wanted to tell them about the wonderful artist Pisanello, who had come specially from Verona to make portrait medals of the Marquis and his family — with what incredible skill and exquisite delicacy the man had contrived to convey each likeness within the tiny circumference of the gold circle. Her father only grunted glumly: "One needs money for that sort of thing."

It was the same with everything else that had been discussed so incessantly at Master Vittorino's school. The brilliant new idea which the Genoese artist, Alberti, had just put forward in his treatise on painting — it gave a depth and naturalness to a picture, so that in the case of a street scene you had the extraordinary feeling that you could walk *into* it. "Perspective" her teacher called the idea. But her father merely laughed and said, "If he painted anything like that on our wall, I'd be afraid of bumping my nose."

Whether it was art or literature or science, some fresh

and revolutionary theory or an exciting rediscovery of ancient Greek wisdom, what had thrilled her at Mantua left her parents quite unmoved. She gave up the effort.

There was no one else in San Stefano, old or young, with whom she could truly communicate. Even the priests, whom she had respected as men of learning when she was a child, now appeared to her as timid and ignorant, rooted in the past, sniffing heresy in the slightest attempt to ask questions and discuss.

She could not even escape into books. At Mantua she had discovered the infinite joys and consolations of reading. For those three years she had feasted on Roman and Greek literature, on the great Italian authors, Dante, Petrarch, Boccaccio, and the rest, and on the romances of French chivalry. But here at San Stefano, where she needed books far more desperately, there were really none – only psalters, a volume or two of dull chronicles, and the one book she had ever seen her father open, the Emperor Frederick's treatise on falconry. Books were expensive. Copied by hand – how could they not be? And in a home where there was no respect for the written word it was unreasonable to look for them. But oh, how she longed for the crowded presses in the library she had left behind.

Above everything, she missed the laughter and gossip of Mantua. I miss, she admitted to herself, even that pious little cat, Anna. But Margherita Gonzaga especially, and her elder sister, even though Cecilia's intellect had been alarming at times. And of course the boys . . .

She had got over Federigo. It had been, she now assured herself, just the sentimental adoration of a small girl for a big boy. There had been one or two other boys after his departure – her heart had fluttered briefly but violently, but she had never again felt the desperation of that first passion. She often thought about Federigo, but quite coolly, just wondering how he fared. He had gone off to learn the trade of soldiering under one of the foremost condottieri, Piccinino, the Duke of Milan's general. And within six months of marrying Gentile Brancaleone! *I* shouldn't have liked that, Caterina reflected. Perhaps, though, Federigo would not have left her to go campaigning so early in their married life? They said that Gentile was plump. Perhaps Federigo did not care for her. It was just one of those marriages that parents arranged without considering their children. Gentile had produced no baby so far. Caterina felt sorry for her, but confident that she herself would have done better for Federigo. She could not stop her idle mind from straying to such thoughts, though she had got the infatuation out of her system by now, and looked back upon the business of the love-potion and the horoscope with a mixture of secret shame and amusement.

She had liked most of the boys at Mantua . . . almost all of them, in varying degrees, except that odious Taddeo Tregani. Where was *he* now? The last news that had filtered through to his schoolfellows was that he had become a mercenary soldier and taken service with Sigismondo Malatesta of Rimini. A fitting choice . . . The Lord of Rimini was a notorious young villain, only a few years older than Taddeo. They should have a lot in common.

Apart from Taddeo – and Master Vittorino had finally seen through him and told him to go – they had been a wonderful crowd of boys, and they grew more attractive in her memory as the lonely winter months dragged by at San Stefano. Of course, even in the enlightened atmosphere of the Mantuan court, there had been conventions to observe, and the girls had been expected to keep to themselves in many respects. There had been that boy Sandro, the merchant's son, who sat in front of her and turned round with such a charming grin when she whispered some joke in his ear. Now *he* was an amusing devil, she thought wistfully, *he* was one I'd have enjoyed knowing better. But it had never been easy to have real conversations with those you met in class, and all her efforts had been directed at Federigo or some other boy in whom she was temporarily interested. There just had not been time for every one.

Yawning her head off with boredom in the echoing rooms at San Stefano, she thought wryly of the days when there had been a choice of company. By the end of that first winter at home she would have raised a cheer at the sight of any fresh face, male or female, if its owner could read and write and were under thirty.

She was pleased enough when, one bleak day towards the end of Lent, her father came limping stiffly across the stable-yard with an opened letter flapping in his hand.

"We shall have visitors after Easter, as soon as the roads are fit to travel on! Luciano Sorbolo, one of my oldest friends."

Luciano came from the neighbourhood of Gubbio, in the southerly part of the Montefeltro domains. He did not – to Caterina's delight – come alone. Besides his wife, Lapa, and a cavalcade of servants to sustain his dignity, he brought his nineteen-year-old son, Roderigo.

If Caterina did not raise a literal and audible cheer at seeing Roderigo, it was due to her self-control rather than to any lack of enthusiasm.

At first sight Roderigo was entirely admirable. He had the regular features of an antique sculptured hero, with silky corn-coloured hair sweeping almost to the shoulders of a particularly gorgeous vermilion doublet. He rode into the piazza at his father's side on a superb white stallion, with two silvery grey hounds loping devotedly behind.

At the end of their week's stay Caterina's high opinion of both horse and hounds was in no degree diminished.

Roderigo was a different matter.

Physically, he was as splendid a specimen as the well-bred animals he had brought with him, about which he was fluent and knowledgeable. She willingly deferred to that knowledge, and, having a keen interest herself in dogs and horses, found no difficulty in talking, or rather listening to him, that first evening.

By the third day, when they had exhausted the kennels and stables, and Roderigo had dropped some rather tactless remarks about the age and quality of her closest four-footed friends, Caterina began to wish that his conversation extended to other topics.

The Greeks he despised as a weak-kneed lot who seemed unable to stand up to the Turks. When she pointed out that she meant not the modern Greeks in Constantinople but the ancient ones, Homer and the rest, he could not see why she should be interested in them and scarcely listened when she tried to explain. The Romans, he admitted, had been good fighters. Even so, they had been dead a long time, hadn't they? Latin was for priests.

Swallowing her indignation – for she quickly realised that Roderigo did not like girls who argued – she assured him that Mantua had not been all classical studies. She told him of the gay life there and he brightened. Mischievously, she spoke with admiration of Federigo. Here at least she and Roderigo found themselves on common ground. The two young men had met at court in Urbino.

"He's a good sort," Roderigo conceded, "and he's tough all right. That gentle manner is misleading. Pity *he's* not the Count's heir. Don't tell any one I said that," he added hastily. "I'm sure young Oddantonio will do excellently when his time comes to take over."

From the conversation of the older men at dinner it sounded as if this time might not be distant.

"Didn't much like the look of the old Count," said Luciano. "We paid our respects, of course, coming through Urbino."

"We're none of us getting any younger," Caterina's father agreed.

"True. But I'm not talking of aches and pains. Guidantonio is a sick man. He's losing grip. Which might be a temptation to that uncomfortable neighbour of yours."

"Malatesta?"

"Who else?"

"That terrible boy," said Caterina's mother with a shudder.

Caterina smiled privately. To her mother Sigismondo Malatesta was still "that terrible boy", though by now he must be in his mid-twenties. He'd ruled Rimini since he was fifteen, when he'd scornfully thrown off the guiding hand of his regents. Even before that, at thirteen, he'd led his troops in battle. For the last few years he'd been pulling down his ancestral home on the Adriatic shore and replacing it with a stupendous new fortress, the Castel Sismondo, from which he could defy his enemies. And those enemies were numerous. Not only had he shown himself, as Roderigo's father said, "an uncomfortable neighbour", fond of raiding the adjacent territories, but his personal life was a scandal. He was a byword for cruelty and lust, a heretic, a mocker of God, a monstrosity.

"That poor wife of his," said Caterina's mother. "I am positive he poisoned her because she did not give him a child. You'll see. He will be married again within the year – if any parents are so heartless as to give him their daughter."

With only twenty or thirty miles of mountain country between Rimini and Urbino, it was worrying to have such a fearsome character on one's doorstep and one's own ruler in no fit state to fight a campaign.

"But we must not meet trouble half way," said Luciano, to change the subject. "Perhaps this charming daughter of yours will treat us to a song?"

Caterina fetched her lute and sang the songs she had learnt at Mantua. One went to a lilting dance tune, another was a sentimental love lyric, and the third (which she herself liked best) was a ballad about a fat girl going to get herself weighed at the mill, in which different characters answered each other:

"'How very fat you are, dear girl!'
'For that may Heaven blast you, churl!'"

The two older men enjoyed the simple humour and laughed most gratifyingly. But the effect of her performance on Roderigo was deeper. He was sufficiently moved to whisper to her afterwards, "You sing beautifully. But then, you *are* so beautiful."

Caterina was pleased to be called beautiful, especially by so delectable-looking a young man, but over the next two or three days it became monotonous. Roderigo developed a habit of sighing, "You are so beautiful," in a fervid undertone whenever he could get near her, but he seemed incapable of expanding that simple statement. As a four-word refrain, repeated at intervals, it was all right, but she would have liked a little more variety and detail. Roderigo often boasted that he was better at action than at words, and as a would-be lover he lived up to his claim. For the remainder of his week's visit he grew increasingly amorous and Caterina was continually having to detach herself from his clutches. In theory she was not supposed to be alone with him, but with no other young people in the palace it was not practicable to keep within sight of parents or servants every minute of the day.

She made no very sincere effort to avoid his first kiss. He was, after all, extremely attractive to the eye, and after that deadly boring winter she was in no mood to be over particular. She was curious, she would have felt tantalised and cheated if she had missed the experience. But it was a disappointing experience, not as exciting as she had expected, though Roderigo seemed to find it so. He was clumsy, he grew rough, and her lips were quite bruised afterwards. It was not the last kiss they exchanged before the visit ended, but she would have given him more opportunities if she had liked him better.

When the Sorbolo cavalcade had disappeared up the valley, real discussion could begin between Caterina and her parents. It was a warm one.

"We can now tell you," her father began rather pompously, "that we have been talking of your possible engagement to Roderigo."

She was not in a docile mood and his tone irritated her. "There's no need to *tell* me, Father. I'm not completely stupid."

"He liked you," said her mother soothingly. "He liked you very much."

"So I noticed," said Caterina darkly.

"I hope you didn't let him take any improper liberties —"

"No, Mother, you needn't worry –"

"He's a fine young man," continued her father, impatient of the interruption. "Some day San Stefano would be very safe in his hands. I was very glad to hear he'd had some military experience under Colleoni – a sound general, Colleoni –"

"But I am not an army to be commanded, Father."

"Let me finish! In other ways it would be a most suitable match. His parents thoroughly approve of you –"

"I'm obliged to them!"

"They will not make difficulties about too large a dowry. As you will bring San Stefano into the family when I am gone, they are quite prepared to settle for a few thousand florins now – we have still to fix the details but it is all extremely amicable."

"I'm glad of that."

"I don't think we could have hoped for anything more satisfactory. A young man of honourable parentage – his blood almost as good as ours –"

"*And* bone, Father. Sometimes, talking to him – trying to talk to him – I wondered if he wasn't solid bone."

"Didn't you *like* him?" cried her mother incredulously.

"I'm glad somebody's asked me that – at last. He'd be all right if he had two more legs. I mean, I grant you he's well-bred and strong and healthy and good-looking – if he were a horse or a dog I'd have nothing against him. But as a human being! Oh, can't you *see*, either of you? He's stupid. I just found him a terrible bore."

"But, darling, you gave no sign –"

"I am supposed to have some manners, Mother. One tries not to make it obvious that one is bored with a guest. Or to run whispering to one's parents while he's still under the same roof."

"Oh dear, this makes a difference, Piero."

"It makes no difference at all." His face darkened with the rush of angry blood. "Caterina will take the husband I think suitable for her. I did not send her to Mantua to pick up all these high-falutin ideas – you don't get married to sit with your husband talking about art and philosophy. It's time the girl was wedded and bedded and some commonsense knocked into her. What she needs is a man."

"Like San Stefano, I suppose?" Caterina was as flushed as her father. "Is it my happiness we're discussing, or the future military defence of this – this tumbledown survival of family vanity?"

For a moment she thought he was going to strike her. But his hand dropped to his side again. "They taught you too many fine words at that school," he said heavily. "But I shall teach you something you have forgotten. Obedience."

"You can draw up as many marriage contracts as you like. You cannot make me marry someone I don't want to."

"No. But, so long as I live, I can stop your marrying anyone else." For some moments they stood glaring at each other. "And you know the only alternative. You do not strike me as a girl who would wish to end her days as a nun."

That pierced her armour. She had no answer. She could only storm from the room in furious tears.

The following week, which should have been idyllic now that perfect spring weather had come to the Marches, was for Caterina a greyer, more dismal season than the winter months that had gone before. She did not enjoy family disputes, but she could see no way, barring abject surrender, to make up the quarrel.

It was an outside event which suddenly and drastically drew the three of them together again.

She heard her father bawling urgently from the courtyard. Servants were rushing to and fro, leading out horses, staggering under weighty boxes. Her mother was stuffing jewels into a casket.

"Darling! Where have you been? I looked –"

"What on earth is happening?"

"We have to go at once – to Urbino. Gather up your clothes –"

"But, Mother –"

"Malatesta!"

Her father hurried in as fast as his stiff joints nowadays allowed him. At sight of his tense expression Caterina knew that this was no moment for argument. The few words he flung at her were enough. Armed men had been sighted on the skyline. They looked like the forward patrols of a much bigger force.

She knew they must be hostile. Friendly troops would have given ample notice and requested right of way through the San Stefano territory. This could mean only an attack by Malatesta of Rimini. She flew to pack her most treasured possessions, and her father limped after her, urging haste. She could not help asking, over her shoulder:

"Must we go? Can't we bar the gates?"

"Malatesta would take his revenge on the country around. No good saving the town if he burns the farms and destroys the crops."

She saw that. The town lived on the land surrounding it. If the cattle were driven off, the vineyards and orchards hacked down, the sprouting corn trampled, there would be famine in San Stefano and it would take years for the district to recover.

"Nothing for it," her father panted. "We can't fight him. We can only open the gates and pray to God that he'll let the town off lightly."

"But we are going to Urbino?"

"We must. For your sake."

She made no protest. She remembered Malatesta's reputation. A monster, from whom no girl was safe. If her father had been fit to put on his armour, if he could have mustered a strong enough force to man the battlements, she would have taken courage from him and tried to rise to the occasion. But if there was to be no resistance, if the Lord of Rimini was to ride unopposed into San Stefano and plant himself triumphantly in this very house, it would have needed the spirit of a martyr to remain.

She was not that kind of heroine. With trembling fingers she bundled together some clothes and followed her parents downstairs.

As they rode up the valley she looked back and saw the northern ridge pricked with stars of flashing steel as Malatesta's riders advanced into the sun.

CHAPTER NINE

Encounters in Urbino

"WE'RE too late," said Federigo, reining in his horse on the crest of the ridge.

Sandro followed his gaze, across the valley at their feet, to the tight pack of houses clinging to the sides of the crag.

"See those banners?" Federigo said. "Even at this distance I know the colours. Malatesta's, I'm afraid."

"Then Caterina –"

"She may have got away. We'll soon find out."

They had had no later news since leaving Brescia. They had made straight for San Stefano as soon as Federigo had gained his discharge from the Milanese service. Then, by forced marches, they had crossed the Lombard plain, ridden down the old Roman Via Emilia, and turned off into the mountains by the shortest route.

Sandro had found it hard going but he had managed to keep up. The soldiers were rough but friendly, and ready to offer a helping hand. They came from every part of Italy, some from beyond. There were several Germans, a couple of Gascons, a Breton, a Fleming, even a red-haired Scotsman. One thing united them, loyalty to their captain and each other.

He saw that they adored Federigo. He was free and easy, yet, young as he was, he had an air of authority.

He addressed the soldiers as "gentlemen", which Sandro privately considered a flattering description, or as "my honoured brothers". And somehow the crudest of them responded and made an effort not to disappoint him.

"Let's go down and reconnoitre," said Federigo, "but be ready for trouble."

Leaving the main body dismounted on the ridge, he led the way down the wooded hillside with his usual small group of officers and messengers. Riding as one of his cavalcade, Sandro was conscious of a heightened tension in himself, an acceleration of his pulse. For the first time he was advancing into what, at any moment, might develop into action.

The countryside was reassuringly – perhaps deceptively – peaceful. In the distant fields men and women could be seen at work. Federigo turned his head to comment that he saw no sign of wanton damage. There were no charred ruins of house or barn, no hacking down of vines or olive-trees, no trampling of young corn. There were cattle and sheep to be seen. So there had been no wholesale plundering by the enemy.

"A bad sign, in one way," said Federigo.

"How?"

"Malatesta is making more than an ordinary raid. He thinks he is here to stay – that he can add San Stefano to his territories. We'll see about that."

They were well down the hill before they met any one to speak to. A forester answered Federigo's hail and, after a moment's hesitation, came running to the roadside, hat in hand.

"Have you seen any of Malatesta's men today?"

Federigo looked down at him keenly. Watching, Sandro felt sure that the forester was telling the truth. Federigo too seemed satisfied that there was no immediate danger of attack by an enemy patrol. He went on to the question Sandro was dying to ask.

"What happened to Piero Spinelli? And his family?"

"They got out in time, my lord. They went to Urbino."

There was no criticism in the man's tone. If you were one of the "great people" – even if you were only a very minor "great person" – you would have been a fool to stay. Poor folk like himself could only bide where they were, let wars roll over them, and pray to the Saints for protection. But if he had owned another house in Urbino, and had a lovely daughter like the young Lady Caterina, he would have behaved exactly as the Lord Piero had done.

Federigo asked more questions and got the situation clear. There had been no attempt at useless resistance and so both the town and its surrounding countryside had been spared. Of course, there had been isolated atrocities – what could you expect with soldiers? But the Lord of Rimini had hanged two of his men as a warning, and since then they had behaved themselves surprisingly well. No, the Lord of Rimini was no longer in San Stefano. He had ridden off with his main army, leaving a garrison of – two, three hundred? The forester could not say just how many.

"Thank you, friend. Tell your neighbours not to be down-hearted. This is Montefeltro country. My father will see that it remains so."

They rode forward again, came right down to the floor of the valley, forded its boulder-strewn river, and advanced for a closer inspection of the town. Sandro felt the same nervous tension returning. They must be visible to the Malatesta sentries on the towers up there. If a strong force suddenly came galloping through that gateway, what could their own small party do but turn and flee?

Knowing how many miles they had already covered that day, he wondered what chance they would have of getting back up the hillside to the main body before their pursuers, on fresh horses, overtook them.

Federigo remained superbly cool and unhurried. He led them for some distance parallel with the ramparts. At some points the rock face was almost as vertical as the wall. He conferred with two lieutenants old enough to be his father. There was much nodding of heads.

It was obvious that such fortifications could not be carried by assault. A siege was equally out of the question. Federigo had neither sappers nor artillery to breach the walls. And his company of horsemen was far too small in numbers to encircle the entire crag and establish a blockade.

"We can do nothing – for the moment," he announced, wheeling his horse. "We had better report to my father in Urbino."

Sandro loved Urbino at sight. Federigo's native city stood high, but from its walls one looked out to a great amphitheatre of even higher mountains. When Federigo had time to show him round, he named each peak lovingly, as if they were his soldiers, and the sonorous syllables rolled off his tongue like trumpet calls: Monte Carpegna, Monte di Montiego, the two horns of the Sassi di Simeone.

The city itself was embowered in the fresh foliage of early summer. "Urbino the Garden," said Federigo softly, "that's what the ancient Romans called it."

"*Urbinum Hortense*." Sandro supplied the Latin. "It was Pliny, wasn't it?"

"It was. So you've remembered something from school!"

Sandro remembered more than the works of Pliny. Knowing that Federigo had his hands full, reporting to the Count, billeting his troops and dealing with other urgent matters, he asked if he could help by seeking out Piero Spinelli and giving him the latest news of San Stefano.

"I wish you would! Give him my compliments, explain the situation, say we obviously couldn't try to recapture the town – and we must discuss the whole business in a day or two. Oh, and – Sandro –"

"Yes?"

"Kiss Caterina's hand for me, and –"

"Any message?"

Federigo chuckled. "Just say that I will drink to her health at supper tonight – at a safe distance."

"A safe distance?"

"She'll understand."

Sandro found the Spinelli family installed in a narrow gloomy old house, a short step from the Count's palace where he himself was lodged with Federigo's officers. The Palazzo Spinelli was sandwiched between the houses of other petty nobility. It had a flight of steps up to its time-worn door and a carved coat of arms over the lintel, so eroded by weather that he could not tell whether it depicted an eagle or a pelican. Like many such town-houses the building consisted mainly of a single abnormally high tower. It must be ideal, he reflected, for defence or for the exercise of the leg muscles, but inconvenient as a home.

Caterina's father received him alone. He must have been a handsome man once. Now he was grizzled and weather-lined. He shifted in his chair, with an occasional wince, as though racked by rheumatism. He welcomed Sandro with respect, as Federigo's representative, and apologised for the cheerless room. "This palace has scarcely been used since my father's day. If I could have entertained you at my real home, you would have seen how we live in normal times." When Sandro repeated this remark to Caterina afterwards, she almost choked.

"It is for me to apologise, sir," he assured her father, trying to match the formal dignity of his tone. "First to present Lord Federigo's regrets for not coming in person —"

"I understand! The illness of the Count."

"And secondly, he asked me to say, for his inability to drive Malatesta's men from San Stefano — for the moment, that is. But the situation of your town is so strong that it needs only a handful of determined men to hold it against an army."

Sandro's cheeks began to redden as he spoke and his voice faltered with embarrassment. He had not rephrased Federigo's words as tactfully as he might. But his own embarrassment was more than matched by Spinelli's. The man plunged floundering into excuses.

"My Lord Federigo must understand that I abandoned San Stefano to save my peasants from useless sufferings ... Had I been ten years younger it would have been a different story ... But I am in no condition to take the field ... See this arm, young man? I can hardly hold a sword ... And — you may not yourself be aware of this — I have no son —"

Somehow Sandro had to halt the flow of shamefaced apologies. It seemed all wrong for this elderly man to be justifying himself to a mere youth.

"I *am* aware, sir," he said gently, "and also that you have a daughter. May I ask, how is the Lady Caterina?"

Spinelli clutched eagerly at the change of subject. He shouted to a servant to fetch Caterina and her mother, and to bring wine and cakes. Sandro explained that he too had been at the school in Mantua.

"*Sandro!* What a wonderful surprise!"

Caterina interrupted them from the doorway, radiant and incredulous, like someone in a sacred picture witnessing a miracle. He bent and kissed the back of her hand. There seemed nothing odd now about the formal greeting. They had last seen each other as schoolfellows. After a year apart they met as young man and woman. But Caterina's warmth soon melted the formality. She showered questions upon him and gave him little chance to swallow the refreshment her father offered.

Sandro had to explain why he had joined Federigo's company. Spinelli then realised for the first time that this youth, though he had attended the Mantuan school and was now lodged in the Count of Urbino's palace, was only the son of a merchant. The atmosphere of the bare room became noticeably chillier. A new stiffness was apparent in Spinelli's demeanour which had nothing to do with rheumatism. Sandro began to feel he had outstayed his welome, though not with Caterina.

"You will come again?" she insisted. "How long will you be in Urbino?"

"That will depend on Federigo – and where the Count wants him to go."

"Any time –" Caterina began, but her father broke in:

"My daughter is now betrothed to Roderigo Sorbolo. A young gentleman," he added with marked emphasis, "of a very well known family."

"He is to be congratulated," said Sandro, keeping his voice level. He would show Spinelli that he had as much poise and as good manners as any one. But he was thankful that, in bending to brush Caterina's hand with his lips, he was able to hide the pain in his eyes.

Back in the Count's palace he had to wait some time for a chance to report to Federigo on his visit.

Federigo had much upon his mind. He was clearly shocked to find the Count in such poor health. Sandro could not help overhearing the exchange between Federigo and his young half-brother, Oddantonio. The latter struck Sandro as spoilt and conceited.

The half-brothers conversed in fierce whispers.

"Why wasn't I told?" demanded Federigo.

"Why should you be?"

"He *is* my father."

"So it is said –"

"Make another remark like that, and I'll–"

"Don't lay a finger on me, Federigo, or you'll be sorry."

"Shall I?" Federigo snorted. "Why?"

"Because you will not be the next Count of Urbino. I shall."

"God help Urbino."

In his heart Sandro echoed the prayer.

He was not the only one in the city to do so during the months that followed.

Count Guidantonio died soon afterwards. He had had his faults, but Sandro, walking in the long file of mourners, black-cloaked, candle in hand, could tell from the faces of the crowd that he had been loved.

His successor promised to turn out a very different type of ruler. He seized on his new power like an irresponsible child turning out its mother's jewel-box. He could hardly wait for a decent period of mourning to go by before demanding hectic celebrations.

"A dreadful little creature," Caterina confided to Sandro.

Federigo's loyalty restrained his criticism. He would

say no more than, "It is a pity my brother did not go to school in Mantua."

Sandro thought the boy slimy. At first the new Count had seemed disposed to be friendly. He had even praised Sandro's good looks. But soon, summing him up as Federigo's man, not to be detached, he had veered away into offensive coldness.

Sandro was glad that the disturbed conditions on the border of the Montefeltro domains kept Federigo's company out of Urbino. Sigismondo Malatesta was always on the prowl, dangerous as the leopards he was said to keep in his half-built fortress. He had already taken San Stefano. Given the chance, he would snatch more territory. To keep him in check, Federigo established his headquarters nearer the coast, and sent constant patrols along the ridges overlooking the sea. It was easy to guess how sickened he was by the conduct of his half-brother. All he would say was, "If I could please myself I'd go back and take service with Milan. I stay here for the sake of the people, and my father's memory. Some one must stand up to Malatesta."

Caterina had not Sandro's excuse for getting out of Urbino. Stranded there, with no foreseeable hope of returning to San Stefano, she found herself drawn into the new court life developing in the palace. That might have been welcome enough, but court life, as understood by Oddantonio, had none of the elegance and intellectual stimulus of Mantua. To be ruler of a state meant, to this odious youth, that he could do exactly as he liked. What he wanted, he expected to take, and woe betide any one tactless enough to ask for payment. Nor did he confine himself to things. He applied the same principle to persons. Too much, thought Caterina, was said about his youth. He was not all that young. Why should his immaturity prevent his leading his troops in battle? He was mature enough to be a menace to any girl he fancied, and even to married women. She herself had been forced to snub him. "I should tell you, my lord," she had said haughtily, "that I am betrothed to Roderigo Sorbolo." She had never expected to be thankful for that excuse.

She wished that Federigo would take his half-brother on a raid against Malatesta. It might be sinful to wish any one's death, but she could not repress the secret thought that it would be splendid if he were killed in a skirmish, so that Federigo could become Count in his place. Little chance of that! Federigo was too honourable to arrange it, as plenty of people would have done.

In fact, Federigo showed no willingness to expose the young Count to the hazards of a campaign. After a while Sandro thought he had discovered why. The Count had a streak of unnatural cruelty, which Federigo must be aware of, having known him from earliest childhood. What the youth would do, given the opportunities of warfare, was something Federigo preferred not to discover. In Urbino there was a limit to his unpleasant propensities. In a village captured from Malatesta he would be capable of horrors.

No, it was better for him to strut about in the palace, playing the pretty tyrant, while Federigo did the real work of holding his domain together. But it made even Federigo smile rather bitterly when the Pope, knowing little of the scandals in Urbino, raised the Count to higher honours by creating him Duke, a title which even his father had never received.

The new régime meant new faces in the palace. Old advisers were disregarded, old officers dismissed. Oddantonio wanted no greybeards telling him what to do. "I am Duke now," he was heard to say, "and I mean to enjoy it."

His court was going to be a gay one. Amusing newcomers were welcome.

Amusement, however, was expensive. He could not run up debts for everything. The Montefeltro territory was not a rich one. There was a limit to what it would yield in rents and taxes. He was squeezing it to the limit. Federigo, sitting by some distant camp-fire, frowned at the news of each fresh tax increase and of the unrest it was stirring up among the people.

His own main worry, as Sandro realised, was the payment of his soldiers. If they were not paid regularly they would make it up by looting, and not only from their enemies. Or they would desert, leaving the country wide open to Malatesta.

"I think I must ask you to go to Urbino," he said, "and see if *you* can make the Duke see reason. He may listen better to you. You can play on your business training. Tell him I could get a contract tomorrow with the Florentine Republic – so many thousand florins down, so many thousand on the first of next month, and so on. There's no worry with the Florentines. They're business men, they strike a bargain, and they pay on the nail. That's how it should be here. The defence of the country comes first. How many banquets and shows will there be in Urbino if I can't hold my troops together?" He smiled apologetically. "Oh, I know you can't talk to him as bluntly as that. You'll have to catch him when he's sober, and be as tactful as you can."

"I should think," said Sandro, "it will be best if I frighten him a little – and flatter him at the same time."

Federigo laughed ruefully. "You have summed him up. Anyhow, do your best. Get us what money you can."

Sandro did not much like his mission, but the men's

pay fell within the scope of his duties and he was just as worried as Federigo. There were consolations, too, about a visit to Urbino. It would give him an excuse to call on Caterina. Her father might not be too pleased, but he could hardly say anything if there was a message to deliver. Federigo obligingly provided the message.

It was all hopeless, really, Sandro told himself in his more realistic moods. But he could not help hoping.

Business before pleasure, his father always said. So, on arrival in Urbino, he cleaned himself up after the journey and humbly requested an audience of the Duke.

He was kept waiting a long time in the anteroom. He expected that. The Duke was never eager to deal with tiresome business. Bursts of cackling laughter from behind the closed doors showed that he was more agreeably occupied with his friends.

Sandro was not prepared, however, for what happened next. The doors opened and a swarthy young man emerged, still laughing, head turned to the company he was leaving. As he swung round and faced Sandro, the amusement died on his lips.

It was Taddeo Tregani.

His eyes narrowed. "What are *you* doing here?"

Sandro was learning to give nothing away. "I am in the Duke's service now." That could mean much or little. Let Taddeo find out for himself what scant favour he enjoyed at court. "I might ask you the same question," he went on coolly. "When I last heard, you were at Rimini. Fighting for Sigismondo Malatesta."

"You heard that? Well, it's no secret." Taddeo looked faintly uncomfortable none the less. "I couldn't go on serving a monster like that. The man's a fiend. I mean –"

"Your scruples do you credit." Privately, Sandro thought Taddeo was blustering. He wondered what the truth of the matter had been. It was more likely that Malatesta had dismissed Taddeo. What more natural than that Taddeo should then come to seek his fortune in Urbino? Professional soldiers were always changing sides. Taddeo was an opportunist if ever there was one.

A petulant voice spoke from the doorway. "I am ready to receive my brother's messenger." Flushed and suspicious, the Duke was peering at them.

"A thousand pardons, my lord," said Taddeo. "I forgot myself – it was such a delightful surprise, meeting so old a friend."

I am sure it was, Sandro told himself amusedly. Yet how could one survive without some insincerity, he reflected, as he kissed the boy's hand with every sign of respect?

CHAPTER TEN

A Long Night and a Long Ladder

"That young man again," said Caterina's father after Sandro had visited them.

"He brought a message from Federigo," she reminded him.

"A message?" His hairy nostrils flared scornfully. He looked, she could not help thinking, like a scraggy old horse shying at something suspicious in the road. "A message to say nothing. He's no nearer turning those scoundrels out of San Stefano."

"He's the only hope we have, Father."

The long absence from home was getting on their nerves. Spinelli missed his country pastimes. He missed, too, his rents and revenues. Though this house in Urbino was his own, he felt like an exile, and an impoverished one at that. Inevitably his wife and daughter suffered.

Caterina would have enjoyed court life under the old Count, simple though it would have seemed after Mantua. But his successor had no use for elderly country gentlemen with empty purses. Pretty girls were different. She knew, without any vanity, that she could be sure of her own welcome in the palace, but instinct warned her that it was safer to keep away.

"I don't like the way that young fellow looks at you," said her mother.

95

"The Duke?" Caterina was following her private thoughts.

"Who said anything about the Duke? No, no – this Sandro."

"Just what I was thinking," Spinelli agreed. "Not the thing at all. He knows you're going to marry Roderigo."

"Am I? Roderigo seems to have cooled off since we came here!"

"He can't be up and down to Urbino every week. Anyhow, it's not usual to see much of the girl before the wedding. Naturally, his family prefer to mark time until they see how matters develop – "

"Whether we are going to get back to San Stefano, you mean." Caterina was in two minds about it: at least their misfortune was delaying a marriage for which she felt little enthusiasm. "Well, I told you – Federigo's the only hope. And Sandro is our link with him."

"So long as he's only that."

"He shouldn't presume on it," said her mother.

"I grant you," said her father generously, "he looks quite the gentleman. You can't smell the shop. But of course he hasn't the blood."

"I prefer brains," said Caterina tartly. "He's the only person I ever see who is worth talking to. And I think you might have offered him a bed while he is in Urbino, not left him to lodge in that stinking inn."

Her parents exchanged glances. "It would have been . . . unsuitable," said her mother hesitantly.

Sandro had chosen the inn rather than the quarters he might have asked for in the ducal palace because he preferred to be independent. He might have to stay some time in the city. It was hard to get the Duke's serious attention for two minutes together. His mind, when not fogged with liquor, was bent on the planning of some riotous party or the pursuit of a girl. When Sandro did contrive to slip in a word about the soldiers' pay, he turned sulky. He was unwilling to allocate funds that he preferred to spend on his enjoyment. His new courtiers encouraged him.

Among these, Taddeo Tregani was firmly established in favour. That too was no help to Sandro. It was another reason to stay at the inn.

Those were lonely days. Winter had come. He had no friends in the city except Caterina, and, sensing her parents' disapproval, he did not dare to call upon her. Each morning he asked for an interview with the Duke. Secretaries and servants fobbed him off with excuses. When at last he managed to reach the youth's presence he was met with a cold stare from those small pale eyes, a warning to go carefully.

"You must not become a *bore*, Master Vettori." The Duke turned away and called to Taddeo.

Pacing the city walls, cloak-wrapped against the wind whining across from the snow-dappled peaks, Sandro thought sadly how different life in Urbino could have been in happier circumstances. The setting *was* superb, it could still have been Pliny's "Garden City" of long ago. But the violent conditions of more recent ages had crowded it with blank-faced towers and cumbrous masonry. The Palazzo Spinelli was just one grim mansion among many. As for the old Montefeltro palace, not all the gaieties devised by its unattractive new master could brighten its shadowy rooms and passages.

The whole city, but above all the ducal palace, needed opening up. A breath of air, a flood of golden sunshine . . . There were moments when, in his impatience, he would have liked to tear the walls apart and make windows with his own hands. A titanic fantasy! There came

97

back to him that conversation he had once had with Federigo at school. Federigo's boyhood dream of building a palace like the one at Mantua, but on a mountainside like this, a "castle in the air". What a hope! And yet – he could understand now why Federigo's voice had thrilled – *what* a hope. A hope worth entertaining, a great conception, however tiny the chance of fulfilment . . .

One morning he was lucky enough to meet Caterina. She was going home from Mass, an old maid-servant following doglike at her heels. They could only speak briefly. "Maria won't feel she has to say anything about *you*," said Caterina confidently. "I can handle her." Her mother, she explained, would not let her go out, even to church, without an escort. Luckily, her mother did not like the steep lanes and flights of steps leading to San Francesco, so Caterina had developed a special affection for that place of worship and might be found there every morning at the same hour.

Sandro took the hint. They were able to have a longer conversation the next day, moving round the church and pretending to study the frescoes while Maria dozed behind a pillar.

He explained the growing urgency of his mission. Somehow the Duke must be made to face facts. "Can't your father do something? If Federigo has to take service elsewhere, you won't see your home again."

"I don't think Father carries much weight with the Duke." She hesitated, then went on reluctantly, "He'd take more notice of me."

"Who wouldn't?" he muttered, so low that she pretended not to hear.

She sighed, thinking of the young Duke's vicious features and intrusive hands. "I'll do what I can," she said.

*

"How did you manage it?" he demanded, between delight and anxiety, advancing the next morning from the dark side-chapel in which he had been lurking till the service was over.

"You've heard something already? He's really kept his word?"

"The treasurer told me last night. I can have the money tomorrow. The escort will be standing by, and I'll be off before the Duke changes his mind. Bless you, Caterina! Federigo will say the same."

"I did nothing, really." She did not mention – she would have liked to forget – how she had fluttered her eyelashes at the Duke and not snatched her hand away when his heavily-beringed fingers moved stealthily over her own. "I got Father to call upon him. I went along and added my persuasions."

"You did the trick evidently."

"Taddeo helped."

"That's odd."

"He's very bitter against Malatesta, you know."

"That's odd, too. You'd have thought they were two of a kind."

"Ah, but 'when thieves fall out' . . . Anyhow, he tipped the scale for me. When the Duke hesitated over the money, Taddeo pointed out that he could get it by raising the taxes again."

Sandro frowned. "He can't go on doing that for ever. He should hear the men grumbling at the inn."

"Well, Federigo has pay for his soldiers – this time! I hope he'll make the most of it." She shivered, not only from the wintry chill of the church. "I don't want to be here much longer." A return to San Stefano, she knew well, might hasten her wedding. She did not look forward to that, but it would be better than staying here in

Urbino, keeping the Duke at bay, perhaps with increasing difficulty. Roderigo might be dull, but the young Montefeltro was depraved. Roderigo was obsessed with animals. Montefeltro *was* an animal, in essence, for all his silks and velvets, his golden chain and jewelled medallion, his ducal dignity.

She said nothing of this to Sandro. It would worry him to leave her here in this corrupt little court.

"We shall do our best," he was assuring her, "but even Federigo can't work miracles."

"I know that."

At earlier meetings they had discussed the problem of recovering San Stefano. Federigo's hope – if he could hold his forces together until the campaigning season reopened in the spring – was to bring Malatesta to battle and defeat him in the open field. Then there would be a peace settlement, and San Stefano would be returned as one of the essential conditions. Malatesta, unfortunately, was a wily general. It would be hard to corner him. But not so hard as to storm an impregnable position like San Stefano.

"Those walls," said Sandro, coming back to the subject. "They must be sixty feet high, we reckoned – and the rock at the base falls away steeply."

"They're not as high as that everywhere," she corrected him. "I know one place anyhow, just below the monastery. It isn't that the walls dip down, but the bulge of the rock comes higher." Her eyes narrowed as she tried to calculate. "The actual wall wouldn't be more than . . . I'm reckoning by the height of a man . . . Five men, perhaps six."

"Say thirty feet?"

"Ye-es. But it might just as well be sixty, mightn't it? I mean, nobody could carry a thirty-foot ladder up there, even without people shooting at him from the battlements."

"Wait." His interest quickened. "*Could* a man get up the rocks to the base of the wall?"

"Oh, I should think so. I've seen sheep grazing. It's steep, it isn't sheer. But, Sandro, a ladder that length –"

"We've sectional ladders." A hint of superiority crept into his voice as he displayed his new military knowledge. "Now tell me . . ." He went on to ask the questions that Federigo would be sure to raise.

"A long night and a long ladder." Federigo leant forward, face alert in the firelight, ticking off the essentials on his fingers. "A friend at the top, with a cord to lash the end of the ladder to the battlements and hold it steady. And a small party of volunteers. You know, Sandro, I think it can be done."

There was an atmosphere of confidence that night in the farmhouse serving the company as winter headquarters. Studying the half-dozen weather-beaten officers sprawled round the hearth, Sandro was aware of a new cordiality. He was no longer just their commander's friend. He had been to Urbino, sorted out this tiresome money problem, extracted twelve thousand florins from the Duke. He was a bright young fellow, worth his place by the roaring fire of olive logs. They were ready to listen to his suggestions.

Federigo's four essentials presented no difficulty. The company had plenty of short sectional ladders – they were standard equipment for any military force – and there would be no lack of men to use them. There would be long nights for another month or more, the moonless ones predictable: time would be needed to cross the intervening countryside unobserved, and the actual scaling of the wall could not be done hastily.

The final, most vital, essential – a friend at the top – had been guaranteed by Caterina. She had provided Sandro with a letter to Matteo Pasolini, bailiff of one of her father's farms. She was sure he would arrange matters. He was absolutely trustworthy. Probably one of his sons would do the job. By all accounts life was proceeding normally in San Stefano and the surrounding district. The country people went in and out of the town upon their normal business. Only the appearance of an armed force would disturb Malatesta's garrison in its relaxed wintertime routine.

"There are a few things we must check carefully," said Federigo, "before we can be sure. And we mustn't give a hint of what we're planning."

Sandro's old respect for him deepened. Since schooldays Federigo's personality had matured rapidly, and it seemed entirely natural that these veterans should take their lead from him. In after times, looking back to that fireside council of war, Sandro was to realise that even then Federigo had already been, in embryo, the commander he was destined to become, loaded with high-sounding titles and honours, Captain-General to the allied forces of Florence, Naples, Mantua and Milan, Standard-bearer to the Catholic Church. His quiet authority and grasp of situation had been there.

The troops were scattered in winter quarters, for no action was normally expected before the spring. They could not be mobilised without news leaking to Rimini. "So," said Federigo, "we shall pretend we mean to ride seawards and raid Malatesta's own territory." He turned to one of his lieutenants, Roberto da Montafio, a wiry Piedmontese with a scarred and pock-marked face masking a genial disposition. "You wish to lead the ladder party? Then you should make the reconnaissance. Sandro had better go with you to see this man Pasolini. The letter was given to him, and he's the one who has talked to Caterina, so Pasolini will know that everything is above-board."

The reconnaissance was carried out four days later. Taking only a single lance as escort, so as to arouse no alarm in the countryside, they crossed the hills and rode cautiously forward into the Spinelli domain. At that season the bleak uplands were deserted. So were the dryly rustling beechwoods clothing the lower slopes. When they saw the farm they were making for, across the last half-mile of vine-terraces and olive-yards, Roberto left the men-at-arms to keep watch and advanced with Sandro alone.

A chorus of dogs brought nervous figures peering. The place looked prosperous enough, as farms went in this region – you could not expect the lushness of the Lombard plain. Barns, stables and cottages stood round the yard. The bailiff's house had a loggia with a view of the town two or three miles further down the valley.

Pasolini was a big, solid man, bald but for the curly tufts of steely-grey above his ears. As soon as they identified themselves as the Lord Federigo's men, he welcomed them heartily. He was just finishing dinner with his family. They must join them, there was no danger. "We don't see much of Malatesta's scoundrels up here," he said. "We soon should, though, if we fell short with our deliveries." When they were served with meat and wine, he broke the seal of Caterina's letter and studied it. He nodded. "We'll speak more of this, gentlemen, when you have eaten." He glanced meaningly at his wife and daughters, his two sons, Giorgio and Filippo, and the servants bustling about with dishes. The conversation was kept general. Conditions were not good, said Pasolini, but

better out here than in San Stefano itself, where Malatesta's garrison terrified the townspeople. The country-
folk were left more to themselves, so long as they paid up
what was demanded. If they didn't, Malatesta's men were
down on them like a wolfpack. Malatesta was screwing out
every penny for the cost of his immense new castle at
Rimini.

"We should all rejoice to see the Spinellis back," said
the bailiff, and the murmur round the table showed that he
spoke for the whole family.

After the meal he took them on foot, through a leafless
orchard to a point where they could stand, screened from
curious observers, and study the face of the crag, clearly
lit up by the winter sunshine. A dizzy-looking place,
thought Sandro. A bird flashed across, high, yet below the
top of the walls, as though to emphasise the vastness of
empty air.

Pasolini pointed out the bell-tower of the monastery,
a convenient landmark, rising directly above the ramparts
at the spot accessible by the shortest climb.

"We have to find it in the dark," Roberto reminded
him.

"I shall guide you to the base of the wall, myself. It will
be a scramble, but it can be done. How many men?"

"Twenty. I could seize the gates with half a dozen, but
there are the ladders to carry."

"Of course. My two sons can go into the town earlier in
the day – quite openly. Every one knows them, they will
be taking farm produce as usual. Only, they will stay inside when the gates shut for the night."

"Fine." Roberto considered. "It would be best if we
timed the affair not too long before dawn. The sentries
will be at their sleepiest. We shall have more time to bring
the main body of our troops down from the hills. And once

we have opened the gates to them we shall want daylight to occupy the town."

"My sons have friends inside, they can hide themselves till then. May I suggest something, captain?"

"Go ahead."

"The monastery bell is rung at six o'clock, to waken the monks for the early service, Prime. At this time of year that gives you the last hour or two of darkness you want."

"The bell would make a good signal."

"So I thought. I will tell my sons to take up their positions when the bell rings. They will let down a rope –"

"A rope?" For the first time Sandro interrupted.

"A rope," said the bailiff. "How else can you be sure you are exactly below them?"

"And it can be fastened to the end of the ladder," said Roberto. "It will help if your lads can pull on the rope while we raise the ladder gently from underneath. It would be tricky otherwise."

Sandro thought he had had an inspiration. "Do we *need* a ladder? If they're going to let down a rope?"

Roberto swore good-humouredly. "We are soldiers not acrobats. How would you like to climb a rope in full fighting gear? And you forget that the battlements jut out. If you think I am going to spin round helplessly in mid-air, like a blasted spider on a thread –"

"I'm sorry," said Sandro humbly.

"It's bad enough on a stout wooden ladder in a place like that. You should try it some time."

"I'm going to. I'm coming with you."

Roberto's jaw dropped. "First I've heard of it! I'm in charge of this operation. I don't know that I want any beginners."

"Let me come! It was my idea. So if anything goes wrong –"

The scarred face broke into a gargoyle's grin. "There's a certain rough justice there! I think the others would see the sense in that. All right, if Federigo says you can."

CHAPTER ELEVEN

At the Ringing of the Bell

THEY fixed a date just before the new moon. The party that rode into Pasolini's farmyard at midnight was nearer thirty than twenty. Federigo himself had come, wishing to check the arrangements before he brought his main force down from the hills.

Pasolini said, "There's just one thing, my lord."

"Yes?"

"I'd no chance to send you warning, but Malatesta is in the town. He rode in, this afternoon. My sons had left here by then."

"How many men with him?"

"Not many. Perhaps twenty lances."

Federigo grinned, a boy once more. "Then it's good news. We might catch the Lord of Rimini himself. Twenty lances, and the garrison? We can deal with them, Roberto?"

Roberto nodded. "If the plan works. The surprise is everything."

They ran over the details again. Malatesta's presence introduced a new factor. If the main gates could be seized and opened without raising a general alarm, Federigo would enter with his whole company and occupy the key positions before dawn broke. With luck, he might surround the Spinelli palace and catch Malatesta before he could rally his men. If the alarm was given sooner, tactics might have to be modified, and Roberto would use his own discretion.

Federigo rose to leave. "Still want to go with them?" he asked Sandro in an undertone.

"Please."

"Good luck, then." Federigo's hand pressed on his shoulder for a moment. The other farewells were quickly said. Federigo and his escort rode into the darkness. The ladder party settled down for an hour or two round the fire. The tension was too great for sleep. The farm was alive with whispers. Pasolini vouched for the loyalty of every man and woman on the place, but only his two sons had been let into the secret. The rest knew only that to-night the Lord Federigo had been there and that some of his men were still on the premises. If they had known what was intended, they would not have believed it.

"It is time to go," said the bailiff, wrapping himself in a hooded cloak.

They stood up and filed out after him. They were lightly armed, just a steel cap and mail shirt, with sword and dagger. Full battle order would have been impossible. They could not have accomplished the stealthy walk across country in the dark, much less the climb.

The ladders were very short and manageable. They were already padded with cloth where they might knock against something and make a noise. Each pair of men-at-arms shared a section, taking turns to carry it. Sandro held a tightly furled banner and had a trumpet slung across his back. These, Roberto assured him, might play an essential role.

In daylight the way to San Stefano had seemed short. Now, moving with infinite caution, they seemed to take an age. When some obstacle lay ahead, the whispered warning had to be passed back down the line. Most of the time the men held their ladders upright, to avoid colliding with their comrades. When they met with overhanging branches they had to tilt the ladders forward, front end slanting up, with due regard for the man ahead.

Occasionally a guard-dog gave tongue. The first time, Sandro's heart gave a sickening bound. For a moment he imagined the whole enterprise ruined. But the man behind prodded him forward. The advance continued. Sandro realised, with a shamefaced smile at his own nervousness, that the garrison would hardly stand to arms every time a farm dog barked in the valley below.

They splashed through a stream, knee-deep. The water was icy. Stones slipped and clonked noisily underfoot. The darkness brightened, above the water, to a glimmer in which neighbouring figures became visible as shadows. Again, common-sense told him that no dozing sentinel in the town would hear or see anything at such a distance.

They came to the base of the hill on which the town stood. Now it was getting really difficult. The road slanting up to the main gates was much too far to their right for them to make use of it. Pasolini led them zigzag up the ragged skirts of the cliff. There were tufts of tussocky grass, clumps of viciously thorned shrubs, treacherous invisible saplings that slanted from the rock clefts and caught the ladders. There were pauses after every few hesitant paces. They climbed slowly and painfully, their progress like the jerking of a tangled string caught on a series of obstructions.

Sandro was thankful he had no ladder. It was difficult enough as it was to get up that rugged slope in pitch blackness. Yet he was equally thankful it was so dark. It hid the fear in his face. It hid the horror in front. He could almost feel the imminent crag, the vertical masonry uplifted to the moonless sky, but he was spared from seeing what he had to climb.

A halt now, longer than the previous pauses. Something wrong? He dared not whisper to the man just above him. Still no move . . . Had the men in front reached the base of the wall? Roberto had warned them, they must not bunch there, they would not have standing room. It would be easier to assemble the ladder if those behind moved up only when required.

It was bitter, crouched here, braced against the jutting limestone. The rocks were cold, like the bones of long-dead men, yet they seemed to have a malign life, as though striving to throw you off their backs, down, dizzily down, into the void from which you had just struggled.

Still no movement forward. A soldier, Sandro told himself, learns patience. He tried silently to shift his weight, to work the numbness out of foot and fingers. To make the time pass quicker he forced himself to think of other things. Mantua, Caterina, Urbino, Caterina . . .

He was so successful that the bell, when it sounded, came as a startling surprise. High overhead it clanged, a thin, metallic, unmusical sound. The notes hung in the upper air and slowly died.

The monks would be rising sleepily from their hard beds, shuffling from dormitory to chapel in a silent file. And here, at the base of the wall, waited another file of men, even more silent.

Sandro peered upwards. He was just in time to see a pale shape floating in the gloom before it came down jerkily and vanished somewhere above him on the crag.

That must be the white cloth which, Pasolini had promised, his sons would tie to the end of the rope so that it would be easier to find in the dark.

A sort of tremor ran down the line of men, a stirring, a

gradual upward movement. For all their care faint sounds were unavoidable. Sandro guessed that the rope was being tied to the top rungs of the first ladder. Now it was being hoisted upright, lifted clear of the ground. The second section was handed up and lashed to the dangling end of the first. The whole party crept up, a few steps at a time, halting while each fresh section was secured.

Sandro was near the end of the file. He had almost reached the final ledge when the whisper was passed down, "No more ladders!" Roberto had played safe and overestimated. They must have brought two sections too many.

A tiny noise, a wooden creak coming eerily from mid-air, indicating that the first man was going up. It was impossible to see anything. The mass of the wall was blacker even than the moonless sky. More creaks as heavy boots moved from rung to rung. Once, the clink of metal.

Sandro heard another whisper. "You next." It was the bailiff. It meant him. Gingerly he scrambled up the last few yards. Pasolini's great hand cupped his elbow, steadying him. He felt the ladder. It rose vertically before his face, hard, cold, firm as a tree. Pasolini's sons must have it tightly roped to the battlements and the soldiers had wedged it below. It was steady enough, yet it was an unpleasant feeling to stretch out one's arm and realise that it stood so well clear of the wall. The battlements must jut out most sickeningly. One really would be climbing straight up into the empty air.

"Careful with that damned banner," a soldier growled in his ear. "Up you go."

Sandro put his foot on the first rung and started. The banner pole, clutched in his left hand, gave him only half his normal grip with those fingers and he had to beware of knocking it against the ladder. The trumpet slung across his back gave him little thumps as he strained upwards, but at least it made no noise. Things were slightly awkward where one section of ladder joined the next. He took extra care.

Thank God for the darkness! The ladder was steady as the rock itself. Secured at the top, it could not possibly fall, even if the wedges slipped an inch or two at the bottom. He told himself that there was no danger, save in his imagination. The precipice was irrelevant. He had only to keep his nerve, to move hands and feet in an orderly sequence. All the same, thank God for the darkness . . . He preferred not to see the height above him or the depth below.

"Tricky bit, here at the top."

With a surge of relief he heard the croaked encouragment. It was the Florentine Lorenzo, Roberto's second-in-command. Sandro felt his knuckles graze on masonry close to the ladder. Two rungs higher, he could place only his toes on the wooden bar, so near was the wall behind. This was where care and balance were vital. A fumbled foot movement could mean disaster. He bit his lip in concentration. A friendly hand gripped his shoulder, holding him. Another hand relieved him of the banner. With a silent thanksgiving to his favourite saints, he stepped on to the parapet between two of the square merlons, and dropped lightly to the sentry-walk inside.

Up here, under the open sky, he could just make out the blurred shapes of half a dozen men. Roberto must have already taken a party to seize the main gatehouse. That had to be done without the waste of a moment. Everything depended on it. And on Federigo being ready with his main force outside. If the plan broke down on either of those two points, it broke down completely.

The last of the volunteers came over the battlements.

Now they had only to wait, shivering on the paved sentry-walk, peering at the vague rooftops of the town, listening to the muffled chant of the monks in the chapel near at hand. The voices ceased, the service was over . . . Still no sound or signal from the gatehouse . . . How much longer?

Eastwards, Sandro detected a growing pallor in the sky. Soon he could make out the rugged outline of the castle above. A cock crowed, startling him with its vibrant call. It was taken up from a hundred roosts in the sheds and yards of the close-packed town. Somewhere a lantern twinkled yellow. The townsfolk were stirring too.

It seemed strange, after that night of whispers and stealth, to hear ordinary tones and undisguised footfalls. Two men were coming along the ramparts. "Wait," Lorenzo whispered. They all crouched, squeezing themselves into the embrasures. The steps came nearer, then halted. Sandro could hear only the breathing of the soldier pressed against him and the hiss of a dagger drawn from its sheath.

"Who goes there?"

The challenge was arrogant. The sentry could have expected no one more dangerous than a nightwalking thief.

"Get them!" said Lorenzo.

The huddled shadows came to life like giant bats disturbed. But they were too late to prevent the giving of the alarm. The two sentries ran for the doorway of the nearest turret. There were sounds of a struggle as the first of Lorenzo's men caught up with them. There was not much room for movement in that narrow space. Sandro could not see what was happening in front. He heard Lorenzo's sharp order:

"No! You won't catch him now. And we must keep together."

One sentry, it appeared, had held the doorway while his comrade had gone racing down the steps of the turret. Then he had promptly surrendered. He stood now, meekly, a dagger at his throat, while his hands were bound. Some one was grumbling that they should not be bothering with prisoners at a time like this. Lorenzo cut him short. "You know Federigo! You'll answer to him if you harm a man who surrenders."

A bell began to ring. This time, though, it was not the monastery bell. It sounded with an urgent brazen clamour, calling men not to prayer but to arms. Lorenzo swore.

"That's done it. In God's name, what is Roberto doing?"

He had his answer a moment later. From the opposite direction, from the main gatehouse a quarter of a mile to the right, a furious hubbub arose, which almost at once gave place to wild cheering. The cheers were answered by a swelling chorus of trumpets from the misty valley.

"Federigo's there," said Lorenzo. "And Roberto must have occupied the gatehouse. God be thanked!"

It was their own signal to move. Filippo Pasolini pointed along the ramparts to the left. With every moment the grey light was strengthening, disclosing the layout of the town. "You want the Palazzo Spinelli now? This is your quickest way."

He led them at a jog trot. At this point the walls began to slant upwards to the next corner bastion, conforming to the levels of the town. There was a long flight of steps. They panted to the top. The eastern sky reddened. The light rippled on their mail, turned their drawn swords into flashing streaks.

At the top of the steps they were still far below the castle ruins but very near the palace. They could look straight down into the piazza, now milling with armed men. After the sounding of the alarm, there had been no hope of catching Malatesta in his bed. But the essential objective had been secured: Federigo was inside the gates.

"So there will be a proper fight," said Lorenzo grimly. He thought for a few moments, studying the scene below. "Unless we can still give Malatesta a surprise. They say he can be frightened easily. He doesn't like odds against him."

"There he is," said one of the soldiers, pointing down. "We should have brought a good crossbowman!"

Sandro peered curiously at the tall figure hurrying down the steps of the palace. Sigismondo Malatesta was in full armour except for his helmet, though the smooth sheen of his hair gave the impression, in the dawnlight, of a metallic cap. He was too far away for Sandro to distinguish the famous predatory nose and reptilian eyes.

His war-horse was led forward. He climbed into the saddle. He was shouting and gesticulating, marshalling his troops into some kind of order. Meanwhile, coming rapidly nearer, a steady murmur of voices showed that Federigo's men were moving up through the town against little resistance. It was in the piazza that the issue would be decided.

Lorenzo had made his own decision. "Time *we* did something. Give me that trumpet." Sandro unslung it. "When I sound it, hold up the banner – make all the show you can. Spread out, the rest of you. I want to see you all along the wall. But careful – his men have bows if we haven't. And howl like all the fiends in Hell. I want enought noise for a hundred."

He raised the trumpet to his lips and sounded the attack. The others, strung thinly along the sentry-walk, burst into a blood-chilling chorus. Sandro lifted the Montefeltro banner to flap in the dawn breeze. Like the others, he bellowed "Montefeltro!" with the full volume of his lungs.

It was good to see the upturned faces in the piazza, to see the hastily-formed ranks dissolve into their previous confusion. He could only guess at the expression on Malatesta's features. That shining head was promptly covered by a massive helmet. Malatesta pulled down his visor. For a few moments he continued to shout orders, flinging out his arm to point this way and that, spurring his horse through the mass of hesitant soldiers. A few crossbowmen raised their clumsy weapons and discharged their bolts, but the iron missiles only chipped the stonework or whizzed overhead. Taking their cue from Lorenzo, the Montefeltro men ran to and fro along the sentry-walk, ducking and then showing themselves in fresh places to exaggerate their numbers.

"Watch the stairway!" Lorenzo panted between trumpet-blasts. "They may try – but we can beat them off till Federigo –"

The delirious hubbub in the streets showed that it could be only a matter of moments before a triumphant Federigo burst into the piazza at the head of his company. Malatesta was not the slowest to realise it. Sandro saw him suddenly wheel his horse, followed by a handful of other riders, and force his way roughly towards an archway in the far corner.

"He's running for it," said Filippo Pasolini with a scornful chuckle.

"Running – ?" Sandro echoed.

"The postern gate!"

"Can't we stop him?" Sandro's blood was up.

"Not a hope. By the time you've run round the walls he'll be through the gate and halfway home to Rimini. Aren't you satisfied? Look down there."

116

Sandro peered cautiously. No more crossbow bolts were flying. Some of Malatesta's troops had followed their commander's example and had melted away. The rest were flinging down their weapons as Federigo galloped unopposed into the piazza.

Some one had begun to ring the bells of a church further down the hill. And the first rays of sunrise were laying golden fingers on the liberated town.

CHAPTER TWELVE

The Favour of the Duke

CATERINA was finding life at Urbino more and more difficult.

The Duke complained that she appeared so seldom. Taddeo called at the house to drop hints to her parents of their lord's displeasure. The Duke liked company of his own age. He would excuse Spinelli if his health made late night revels a burden to him, but that was no reason to keep his daughter locked up like a nun.

"But I don't *want* to go, Father," she pleaded. "The Duke's parties are dreadful." She added, lamely: "Roderigo wouldn't like it. I am engaged to him, after all."

"Much interest Roderigo shows, since we lost San Stefano! It wouldn't surprise me at all," said Spinelli gloomily, "if he backed out of the marriage. You might win a better husband if you showed your face at court more."

"Oh, Father!" Had he no idea, in his innocence, she asked herself, of the gossip about the Duke and his friends? A decent girl was more likely to lose her reputation than win a husband if she got into that set. The town was seething with scandal, the people more and more indignant. The Duke's behaviour went from bad to worse. Taddeo seemed to egg him on to fresh extravagance and out-rages.

She still made her morning pilgrimage to San Francesco, head primly bowed, the old servant limping and wheezing a pace or two behind. Usually they were the only worshippers, but she still – hoping against hope – glanced between the shadowy pillars in case Sandro should be waiting for her. It was three weeks since he had said good-bye to her here, full of his wild scheme. What had happened, if anything?

And then, coming downstairs in the candle-pricked gloom of early evening, she heard her father's tetchy voice. "Not *another* message of regret from Lord Federigo?" And it was Sandro's answering: "No, sir, I have brought you something more solid." As she ran forward across the hall there was a thump as he dropped a leather pouch on the table.

"What's this?" Her father fumbled. She saw the iron key in his hand, glinting.

"Your palace at San Stefano, sir – with my Lord Federigo's compliments."

"You mean –"

"Sandro!" She broke into the conversation. "You've done it!"

He kissed her hand. It was all very correct, but their eyes danced to each other in the twinkling candle-light. He turned back to Spinelli, straight-backed, straight-faced, very much the messenger. "The town has been recovered, sir. There was no damage to speak of. Malatesta himself had just spent a night in your own home – everything seems in order, though you may wish to perfume the place –" Sandro allowed himself a gentle chuckle. "Meanwhile, Lord Federigo has locked the door and set a guard – and here is the key."

For once Spinelli was ungrudging in his welcome. Wine was brought. He wanted the details. "You were there, yourself, young man?"

Again Sandro's eyes met Caterina's, and she knew that she could rely upon him to say nothing about their private meetings and her share in the plan. "What did *you* do?" she demanded eagerly.

"Oh," he said lightly, "I just carried a banner."

The Duke's reception of Sandro's report was more critical.

He took the recapture of San Stefano as a matter of course. What else were the soldiers paid to do? He exclaimed scornfully over Malatesta's escape. "What a bungle!" Taddeo, lounging behind his chair, was quick to agree, though Sandro had a puzzling impression that Taddeo had looked anxious at the first mention of Malatesta's involvement in the affair.

"With respect, my lord," he explained, keeping his voice level, "your brother knew about the postern gate."

"Then why wasn't it blockaded?"

"We hadn't the men to spare. We had to get them all inside to overwhelm any resistance. If the garrison saw they had no hope, and bolted through the other gate, so much the better." Seeing the Duke's incredulous face, Sandro continued patiently: "Our main object was not to kill Malatesta's soldiers but to liberate the town. The less fighting, the less damage. Of course, if we had known in time that Malatesta himself was inside, my Lord Federigo might have taken the risk and detached a party to seal off the postern. But we had too little warning. He could not alter his dispositions at the last moment."

The Duke seemed unwilling to grasp the explanation.

He was infuriated by the request – which Sandro introduced as tactfully as he could – that Federigo should be sent the next instalment of pay for his men.

"What do they want with pay? They would get ransom money if they did not let the enemy escape. They did take some prisoners."

"Yes, my lord. Many of the common soldiers surrendered. But their ransom – if we can collect it – won't amount to much."

"Your men have loot. They've captured a town."

"A friendly town. Your brother would never let his men plunder your own subjects."

"Well, *I* have no money for them."

Once more Taddeo surprised Sandro. He bent forward. "You could screw a little more from these fat merchants, my lord."

From his inn Sandro wrote to Federigo. Taking no chances, he used the Greek of their schooldays.

"*There is a bad atmosphere in the city,*" he reported, "*worse than last time. There is even more discontent among the people, and – to speak honestly – there is good reason. The Duke is unfortunate in his advisers. They exploit the fact that he is young, inexperienced and interested only in his personal pleasures. T. especially is his evil genius. He is said to have quarrelled with Malatesta. Yet, if he were still working for Malatesta, he could scarcely do more to harm the Montefeltro interests. Anything that makes the Duke of Urbino unpopular and weakens his government is obviously to Malatesta's advantage. Whether deliberate or accidental, this is certainly the result of this man's influence.*"

Sandro paused, chewed the end of his quill, and then scratched his initials at the foot of the letter. It was not easy to write to Federigo about his half-brother, but the true state of affairs in Urbino was too ugly for him to keep silent. For the present, he had said enough. He could not bring himself to tell Federigo of the Duke's latest atrocity, when he had lost his temper with a page and had the boy burnt alive.

He let the ink dry, folded the paper, and sealed it. What was going to be the end of all this? Would Federigo go on for ever, fighting his brother's battles, propping up a hated government, merely from family loyalty? He could not imagine it, any more than he could imagine Federigo lending himself to some plot – as many a man had done in other cities – to seize power for himself. No, when Federigo and the Duke came to the breaking point, Federigo would withdraw with dignity and sell his sword to a more satisfactory government elsewhere. And Sandro would be happy to go with him, to Florence or Naples, Venice or Milan, wherever Federigo liked.

Happy? But for one thing.

The thought of Caterina nagged at the back of his mind. Her father was waiting only for the spring weather to return to San Stefano. There was renewed talk of her marriage. Roderigo's interest had revived magically, now that the Spinellis had got back their domains. In the summer, probably, when the Spinellis had managed to furbish up their home and get together some money for the celebrations, there would be a grand wedding at San Stefano.

Sandro had met Roderigo. The prospect did not fill him with enthusiasm. The two young men had found nothing to talk about. Roderigo had been slightly prickly because Sandro had helped in the capture of the town and he had not. Caterina had looked bored with him. She would never be happy with such a witless specimen, however presentable his looks and pedigree. What a waste, thought Sandro with a groan.

On the morning after his arrival he had taken a chance and waited in San Francesco. And Caterina had come, Maria like a tactful shadow bobbing at her heels.

Caterina had looked pleased and excited and disapproving all at the same time. "We shouldn't," she had said, and in saying "we", not "you", had given herself away.

"Why not?"

"If any one saw us, they might think . . ."

"What?"

"That we were . . . lovers."

"And then?" He probed mercilessly.

"Father would lock me up to protect my virtue. And Roderigo would feel he had to challenge you to fight."

"Roderigo always does the correct thing."

"You musn't make fun of Roderigo. I am going to marry him."

"You don't need to remind me."

"Don't sound so bitter," she pleaded. She laid a hand gently on his arm. It was not often that they touched. Even through leather glove and velvet sleeve the physical contact set his heart drumming. "Make me laugh, Sandro," she said. "You always used to make me laugh."

He tried, but it was not easy for either of them. The future weighed them down. In a few days Sandro must start back for Federigo's camp, already moved to Pesaro on the coast. When he next had business in Urbino she herself would be gone. Quite likely they would never meet again. Soon she would be a married woman, bearing children to Roderigo. If they met at all, they would not be free to talk like this, alone.

He did not mean to go to San Francesco the next day but the desire proved too strong to resist. Again she tried to look disapproving. "If you really want to avoid me," he teased her, "you would hear Mass in another church!" She laughed and gave up pretending. "What's the harm, after all?" she said. "Meeting you is the one bright moment in these dreary days." They paced the church for as long as she dared to stay, talking of everything but the future. She sympathised with him for these humiliating visits to court but envied the rest of his existence, the days of riding across the hills with Federigo's company, the evenings of good talk at the camp-fires, the men he met and the stories they had to tell.

They had a week of these early morning encounters. On the day after tomorrow he would have to leave the city. The treasurer promised that the money would be ready. He could not delay his going, once his mission was accomplished.

That morning, parting at the church door, careless because the tiny piazza outside seemed always empty, they realised too late that some one was waiting for them. A tall figure stood shadowed in a doorway opposite. He stepped forward, swept off his hat to Caterina with exaggerated courtesy, and wished them good-morning.

"Good morning, Taddeo," she said faintly.

"Church-going – such *regular* church-going – is an excellent habit. Your parents must be pleased. And Roderigo. And they would all be glad to hear that Sandro is equally regular in – shall we say? – the pursuit of virtue."

"Look here, Taddeo," Sandro began, but Caterina laid a warning hand on his arm.

She laughed. "With all the real scandals this city is full of, I'm sure you don't need to work up empty gossip about me." She recovered her nerve. Sandro admired her carefree tone. But then she herself had never clashed openly with Taddeo. In theory they were friends. "Well," she asked, tilting her head with a provocative smile, "are you going to upset my poor old father? Do you have to?"

"Not necessarily." He smiled too. "It depends."

Back in her room, she began to tremble uncontrollably.

What would Taddeo do with his knowledge? Something, she was sure. It was no accident he had met them. He knew of the other mornings. He had spied on them.

Yet, apart from paying off an old grudge against Sandro, what would he gain by telling tales? Suppose he kept his knowledge as a threat hanging over them, a bargaining counter? Her mind considered the various possibilities and flinched from them. Oh, to have Margherita Gonzaga sitting beside her, as in the old days! Margherita would have hit on some way to handle him.

If the story of those meetings came out, Sandro could look after himself. He was a man. It would be hardest for poor old Maria, the trusted servant who in pure soft-heartedness had turned a blind eye to her young mistress's unconventional behaviour. Caterina clenched her fists. Father was capable of turning Maria into the streets. He mustn't. Maria mustn't suffer. At all costs Taddeo must be kept sweet, persuaded not to say the word that would make her father boil over.

At all costs? She groaned. From the past – it seemed a lifetime ago – she heard the insistent voice of Master Vittorino. "Use words exactly, my dear. Think out their full and precise significance before you use them." At all costs . . . How high might the cost go? She thought of the way the Duke looked at her and of Taddeo's reputation – it was Taddeo who hid the Duke's dirty work and boasted (people said) that he could get his young master anything he wanted.

She must pull herself together, wash her face, bathe

her eyes, go downstairs and talk normally to her parents. It would soon be dinner-time. Somehow she would have to swallow her food.

In the ordinary way few outdoor sounds penetrated the massive walls of the house, but now she became suddenly aware of a distant shouting. A bell began to clang. It was taken up by other bells in the city. Craning from the open window-slit at the turn of the stairs she heard the clatter of running feet on the paving stones. The clamour of voices took on a distinct rhythm, became a chorus, hammered out word by word.

Maria was struggling up the stairs, white-faced and breathless. "My lady!"

"What is it?"

"Something dreadful – has – happened –" The old woman stopped. She patted her heaving bosom. "That young gentleman we met this morning –"

Caterina's heart seemed to stop. "Master Sandro –"

"No, no, the other. He is downstairs with your father –"

"Taddeo Tregani?" One kind of fear replaced another. "What does *he* want?"

"He wants us to hide him –"

"For God's sake, Maria, what's happening?"

"The Duke! He's dead! And several of the court with him. They almost tore them to pieces. They'd have done the same to that young gentleman if he'd been in the palace at the time."

Now Caterina could make out the words the crowd were shouting in the piazza. "Out – with – the Monte – feltri!" Her lips framed a silent prayer that Sandro might be safe.

CHAPTER THIRTEEN

The Gates of the City

"You must have ridden that black gelding of yours like the devil," said Federigo. "Sit down, for God's sake. You're exhausted."

Wine poppled golden from the flagon. Sandro curled shaky fingers round the stem of the goblet. He took a drink, then tore gratefully at the crusty bread. Suddenly he realised how long it was since he had eaten.

"Old Naddo was game enough," he mumbled. "I felt you ought to know at once."

"Yes." Federigo's face was set. He had been finishing his meal when Sandro burst mud-spattered into his headquarters. A volume lay open beside his plate, Caesar's *Civil War*. He kept up his reading even on campaign. He dreamed wistfully of some day possessing a permanent library where he could collect in one place all the books there had ever been and enjoy them peacefully with his friends. "You must have something cooked," he said gently, and beckoned to the hovering servant.

It was like Federigo to think of such details, though he had just been told of his brother's savage death. He sat brooding. Then he looked across the table, eyes shadowed with pain.

"God's mercy on his soul," he said. "Poor little wretch! He was a monster, true –"

"You realised that?"

"He was my half-brother. I grew up with him. One couldn't *help* realising. Still, it was a terrible way to die, though Heaven knows he asked for it. They're good people in Urbino, really." He seemed almost to be apologizing. "They must have been goaded beyond endurance. There'll be no talk of revenge, Sandro, no reprisals."

"I hoped you would say that."

"Each act of revenge only breeds another. The pagan Greeks knew that much from their poets. He was my brother, true, but the people who killed him are *my* people."

"What will you do? If Malatesta exploits this –"

"Exactly. Finish your supper and get some sleep. If you're fit to come, you'll be taking the same road back with me in the morning."

Federigo's camp at Pesaro was scarcely twenty-five miles from Urbino. So, thanks to Sandro's promptitude, he could react swiftly to the new situation.

The weather, too, lent itself to movement. Spring had burst out suddenly in the past few days. In any case there were no snow-blocked passes to negotiate. It was a valley road all the way up to the heights on which the city stood, at first along the banks of the Foglia and then winding slowly upwards beside a smaller stream.

The morning was soft. The sun slanted down the up-held lances. The banners flapped like a skein of geese against the cloudless sky. Riding at the head of the column with Federigo, Sandro tried to distract him with talk of personal things. Federigo was always interested in news of Caterina, whom he admired in a slightly amused way.

"She'll be safe enough till we get there," he assured Sandro. "The Spinellis weren't involved in my brother's misdeeds. And they'd be perfectly all right in that gloomy old stronghold they call a house. It would keep out an army, never mind a mob."

Sandro was comforted. That was what he had argued when faced with the instant choice, either to get out of the city with the vital news before the gates were shut, or to forget his duty and appoint himself uninvited protector to the Spinellis. He was encouraged now to confide in Federigo. He began to explain his meetings with Caterina.

"You young dog," Federigo commented agreeably.

"It was all perfectly innocent –"

"I'm sure it was!"

"Caterina was bored and miserable. After all, we were pupils together at Mantua –"

"May I offer you a word of advice, young Sandro?"

"Of course."

"I am sorry if Caterina was bored. But it is not your business to amuse her. I'm no saint – I like the girls, who doesn't? But I don't want you to end up with a knife between your shoulderblades. Caterina is promised to Roderigo. I agree that's a pity. But even if she were not – and even if she wanted to marry you, instead, which you have not suggested –"

"Oh, no," Sandro admitted quickly. "There's not been a hint –"

"I believe that. Others might wonder. But, as I say, even if she were madly in love with you, that father of hers wouldn't have it. He thinks only of ancestors, coats-of-arms. He'd have a fit if he heard you'd been meeting her –"

"That's what is worrying me." Sandro told the story of Taddeo's intervention. To his relief, Federigo laughed.

"Taddeo won't trouble you."

"How can you be sure?"

"If he saved his own skin – and being Taddeo he probably did – he's probably back in Rimini."

"But Malatesta threw him out!"

"I wonder. It could have been a blind. I've heard things while you've been away. It seems that Malatesta had an ingenious idea for weakening Urbino. Given time, my brother would make a mess of things, but Malatesta thought he could accelerate the process. It was a question of planting the right – or wrong – sort of advisers in my brother's court, tempting him into policies that would suit Malatesta."

"That would certainly explain Taddeo's rather odd behaviour," agreed Sandro thoughtfully.

"The man's warped. Even dear old Vittorino had to recognise the fact in the end." They rode on in silence for a little while, the long column jingling behind them. "He's just right for Malatesta," said Federigo. "They're both as twisty as snakes. But we can scotch them. They couldn't have expected events to move quite as fast as this."

In the feverish atmosphere created by the Duke's murder, Caterina had accepted Taddeo's arrival in the house as inevitable. Her distaste for him did not matter. He could not be turned away, perhaps to be torn limb from limb by a raging mob as one of the Duke's most hated favourites. In any case she was in no position to explain to her father why Taddeo's presence under the same roof was unwelcome.

"We must get out of here at once," Spinelli announced. "The city must have gone mad. Appalling behaviour! No place for women and children."

He had been postponing the return to San Stefano until milder weather improved the travelling conditions, but it would be folly to remain any longer in Urbino. No one knew what the people would get up to next. Servants who ventured out into the streets came back with rumours of a republic. Spinelli began to imagine a general attack upon the upper class – a forcible expulsion of families like themselves, if not a bloody massacre. In these alarming forecasts he was warmly supported by Taddeo, who curdled their blood with stories of such happenings in his native Perugia.

They spent an uneasy day and night behind barred doors, making preparations to leave in the morning as soon as the gates opened – if they did open. At such a time even Caterina would have welcomed Roderigo as escort, but her betrothed never seemed to be at hand when most required: he was away on the Sorbolo estates near Gubbio. Taddeo, recovering smartly from the brief panic which had brought him begging for shelter, offered himself as temporary substitute. He too was anxious to get out of Urbino, and could more easily do so if he merged himself into the Spinelli entourage. He had, he pointed out, five personal followers, as trustworthy as they were tough. Their swords, together with his own, should be enough to deter any one who tried to molest the travellers on the open road.

Spinelli closed with the offer enthusiastically, and, to Caterina's concealed dismay, pressed Taddeo to be their guest at San Stefano until he had decided his next move. A servant set forth, traced Taddeo's servants to their quarters, and brought them discreetly to the house under cover of dusk. They were, thought Caterina, a formidable quintet of ruffians. They would certainly frighten off most people. They frightened her.

There was no difficulty about passing through the gates the next morning. The city seemed tense but orderly.

There were more armed guards about than usual, but they appeared less interested in people leaving than in those who might soon arrive.

"They look as if they're preparing for a siege," said Spinelli when they were safely outside.

Taddeo laughed. "Yes. If Federigo imagines he's going to walk in and take over Urbino, he's in for a surprise."

Caterina stared at him, side-long, as they trotted down the road abreast. She said nothing. It was better to hide her disgust. It was no fresh news that Taddeo hated Federigo. It had always been so. For herself, she must handle Taddeo carefully. He was the more dangerous now that he was safe from the citizens. He knew just how to flatter her father, the two of them were getting on famously. Whatever Taddeo might tell him, her father would be ready to believe.

To do him justice, Taddeo seemed anxious now to make amends for his veiled threat yesterday. He was an attentive escort, his manners were impeccable, and he exerted himself to save the family from the petty discomforts and anxieties of their sudden journey. In such private conversations as he had with her, when mountain roads narrowed and they found themselves paired, Taddeo exuded charm.

It was the fascination, however, of the serpent. It left her quite unmoved. God, she thought furiously, as the cavalcade wound its way up towards the skyline, yesterday he accused me of disloyalty to Roderigo, and now, given half a chance, he'd make love to me himself! If he was really going to stay with them at San Stefano, she would take good care never to be in a room with him alone.

"So," said Federigo, "my own people have shut their gates in my face." He reined in his horse and stared at the city, piled up behind its walls, dark on its hill against the lemon sky of sunset. He spoke sadly but without anger.

"We'll soon see about that," Roberto said.

Lorenzo had ridden forward to investigate. Hoofs drummed in the gloaming as he hurried back. "They won't open till they have your word," he told Federigo. "They say there are a lot of points to be agreed."

Roberto swore. "Can't they open the gates and let us in, at least? Discussions should be held in comfort."

"They are quite right," said Federigo. "Would *you* let an army into your town before you knew the terms?"

"It's your city. By right, you're their new duke."

"I am my father's son," Federigo corrected him mildly. "I suppose I am Count of Urbino now, as he was. Whether I am ever Duke depends on His Holiness. And whether I actually rule Urbino, as my family have done for generations, depends on the goodwill of those worthy citizens up there on the ramparts. Not, if you'll forgive me –" he checked Roberto's contemptuous interruption, "on the valour of you and all these other gallant gentlemen. Much as I appreciate it!"

There was nothing for it but to pitch camp for the night, keeping as warm and comfortable as they could in the fields below the city. There was much indignation round the camp-fires, but Federigo was philosophical. To Sandro he talked quietly of ancient history, how Pericles had guided the Athenian democracy by persuasion and the greatest of the Romans had shown respect to the senate. "Some of my friends," he murmured with a glance towards the other officers, "think I am a fool to base my life on what men did so long ago. You were at Vittorino's. Perhaps you understand?"

"I think I do." Sandro hesitated. "If it's done within reason."

"'*Nothing in excess*', as the Greeks used to say?"

"Yes. I agree, there's a lot of wisdom in the Classics. But if they were the last word on Life – well, there wouldn't be much point, would there?"

In the morning the Bishop of Urbino came down into the camp to act as mediator. It fell to Sandro to act as secretary to the conference, noting the demands put forward by the townspeople and summarising them in fair copies on parchment.

There was to be a general amnesty: no action was to be taken against those concerned in the killing of the Duke and his companions. The Duke's debts were to be paid. Taxes were to be cut, there must be reforms of this and that injustice in the government.

Conscious of their own strong position, and encouraged by Federigo's agreeable response, the delegation of townsmen pressed their advantage and asked for new concessions. They proposed a free medical service for all and education for their children. Federigo agreed that two doctors and two teachers should be appointed and paid for out of public revenue.

Sandro's eyebrows went up when he reached the end of the list. "You've promised a great deal," he said. He wondered how Federigo, with the best will in the world, was going to pay off his brother's extravagant debts, increase benefits for the people, and at the same time collect less in taxes. The money would have to come from somewhere.

"I shall earn the money," Federigo said. "With my sword. There are plenty who will be glad to hire it."

"But you can't turn your back on Malatesta."

Federigo grinned. "No. But he's a nuisance to bigger states than Urbino. The Florentine Republic, for instance, or His Holiness in Rome. They need a condottiere to do their fighting for them. I shall take care of Malatesta, they'll pay – and there'll be something left over for Urbino. You'll see." He handed back the document. "We'll embody all these terms in a public proclamation. Then every one will know how things stand."

Later that day they made a formal entry into the city. There was every sign of rejoicing, with bells clanging, people cheering from every balcony, banners streaming in the wind, and brightly coloured cloths hung from the windowsills.

Only the Spinelli mansion was untenanted and unadorned when Sandro hurried there after his duties.

An old man finally appeared. The whole family, he said, had left for San Stefano.

Sandro was disappointed but not surprised. The real surprise came at supper in the Montefeltro palace.

Roberto had been charged with the inquiries into Taddeo's fate. "You guessed right," he told Federigo, "they didn't get their hands on *him*. It was quite difficult to discover just how and when he slipped out of the city. But it now looks as though he went with the Spinellis."

Federigo pursed his lips. "Extraordinary. I don't like the sound of that." Nor did Sandro, but he did not voice the uneasiness that suddenly gripped him.

CHAPTER FOURTEEN

A Fork in the Road

No, Caterina told herself for the third time, evading Taddeo's too ready hands as she slid from her saddle at their overnight halt, he was emphatically not a young man she would care to be left alone with. Fortunately the party had to sleep at a wayside monastery and she shared a guest-chamber with her mother, who pleaded fatigue and went to bed early. By pretending tiredness herself, Catterina was able to avoid Taddeo. She left him drinking with her father.

It was a long time before she fell asleep. She lay beside her mother in the darkness, dismally reviewing her future. Soon, after a few months of choosing materials, stitching, filling her bridal chest and discussing the details of the banquet, she would be lying in another such bed with Roderigo at her side. At least, she tried to console herself, he was better than Taddeo. That was not saying much, but what choice did a girl have?

Taddeo's company was unavoidable in the daytime, but she felt easier beneath the open sky, with the reassuring feel of the horse under her. Mounted, she was in command of the situation. He had to postpone his sly attempts at physical contact, she could ignore his flirtatious compliments and the double meanings that embarrassed her. On the second morning, slipping quickly into the saddle before he could assist her, she resolved that she would ride all day with the erect carriage and downcast eyes of the most demure nun. If Taddeo's conversation became tiresome she would pretend not to hear.

It was a hard resolution to keep. Her nature was not a nun's. She could not suppress her identity. Always her vitality would break through. She was irked by the crawling pace of the little cavalcade, but her parents could not hurry. She could not ride glumly beside them every mile. Either they exchanged no word, like mutes in a funeral procession, or she was provoked to say things she afterwards regretted. Any company seemed, for the moment, more entertaining than theirs.

One of Taddeo's men, Grifone, was quite amusing. A terrible rogue, really, she told herself, but weren't they all? At least his battered features creased into a good-humoured smile and he could tell tall stories with a salty wit that did something to shorten the journey. So long as he was there, she did not mind if Taddeo rode quietly on her other side.

Two more of Taddeo's servants went ahead of the party, continually galloping forward to the next hilltop or bend in the road, and signalling back reassurance that it was safe to come on. In the present state of unrest after the Duke's murder it was impossible to guarantee a safe passage home. Some band of discontented villagers might have risen in revolt or brigands be exploiting the downfall of the government. And there was always the chance of Malatesta's raiders. Even Caterina was glad to have Taddeo's men to strengthen the party, though she would have preferred them under a different master.

The second morning passed pleasantly. The sun was growing stronger, the birds sang. Grifone told the most outrageous tales of his bygone campaigns. He claimed to have served under all the greatest condottieri, Sforza, Braccio, Carmagnola, every general she had heard of. It was hard to stem his flow, and mostly she was happy enough to listen and laugh, but at one point she felt compelled to break in.

"Taddeo! Is this the right way?"

"Of course." He pointed. The two leading riders had reined in on the crest and were signalling that all was clear beyond.

"I'm sorry. I don't remember this bit of the road. Didn't we pass a fork just now? I thought it was the *left* to San Stefano?"

"No, right. You'll see in a moment."

As if to convince her, he set his horse to a trot. Only too glad of a change of gait, she followed with Grifone. They caught up with the two men on the skyline. A whole new prospect opened at their feet. A few miles away the Adriatic spread azure to the horizon. The coastal sands stretched north and south like a brown scarf. At intervals there were compactly clustered towns, like brooches pinned to it. She pointed accusingly to the nearest. It had a conspicuous castle.

"That looks like Rimini!"

"It is," said Taddeo.

"Then you *were* wrong. This isn't the road we want."

"On the contrary. It is the road *I* want."

For a moment the significance of his tone did not penetrate to her. She was concerned only to convince him of his mistake. "No, Taddeo, really –" She turned in her saddle and looked down the hill they had climbed. She could see the fork in the road, her parents and the rest of the party halted there, small as puppets at this distance. Taddeo's two remaining servants had detached themselves and were spurring up the hill. "Look," she said, "your men are hurrying after us to fetch us back."

Taddeo laughed oddly, and then she knew. She tried to turn her horse, but of course it was much too late now. Grifone's hand was on her bridle, and the others were all round her. Not unkindly Grifone pleaded, "Be sensible, young lady. No one wants to be rough."

It was a full week before the news reached Sandro in Urbino. It had been a busy time. Federigo was issuing proclamations, investigating grievances, receiving petitions and declarations of loyalty from the smaller towns and villages, listening to high-flown messages of congratulation from other rulers. Sandro was in the midst of it all, drafting letters, checking accounts, working far into the night to sort out some of the mess left behind by the late Duke's misgovernment.

Some one told him the news casually, not guessing it had any great personal interest. Sandro went white. He dropped what he was doing and ran through the palace to find Federigo.

"My lord!" He had become carefully formal nowadays when others were in hearing.

"My dear Sandro! What –"

"Caterina –"

"Not ill?" Federigo put a steadying hand on his arm.

"That swine Taddeo! He's abducted her!" Sandro stammered out the story as it had been told to him. "Of course, the old man couldn't do a thing – he could never have caught up with them. And they planned it so cunningly." He looked at Federigo in desperation. "What can we do?"

"Sit down." Federigo took a few steps up and down the

room, fingering the gold chain looped across his chest. "What can we do?" he echoed the question grimly.

"We must do something!"

"You say he has taken her to Rimini?"

"Yes."

"Then –" Federigo spread his open palms in a helpless gesture. "Forgive me, Sandro. I know – I think I know – how you feel about Caterina. But if she is inside Malatesta's new castle it would take an army to get her out. I haven't that kind of army."

Sandro jumped to his feet again. It was one of the few times in his life when he came near to quarrelling with Federigo. "So you won't do anything?"

"Not won't. Can't. Unless you can suggest some reasonable move that's within my –"

"I don't feel reasonable!"

Federigo said, gently: "What does Roderigo say? It's – forgive me – it's more his concern than anybody else's."

"I'll see. By your leave, my lord," Sandro added loudly, and flung out of the room.

Roderigo was in the city. He had come with the delegation from Gubbio to swear allegiance to Federigo. Sandro found him raging, but less for Caterina's sake, it seemed, than for the affront to his own dignity.

"He can't do this to me," he repeated. "She was my intended wife – it was all settled."

"He *has* done it," Sandro pointed out brutally. "The point is, what are *you* going to do?"

"I shall send him a challenge."

"Do you imagine he'll accept it? Taddeo Tregani?"

"What else *can* I do, as a gentleman? I have my honour to think of."

Sandro's temper flashed. "You have Caterina to think of."

"Of course! If Taddeo will fight, I shall avenge her honour as well as my own."

"But you know in your heart he will not fight you. So in the end you will accept the situation?"

"I may have to. You don't expect me to tear down the Castel Sismondo with my bare hands?"

"There might be subtler ways of getting her back – if she can't be rescued you might make a deal with him –"

"A deal! Men of honour don't make deals."

"Men of honour pay ransom –"

"It's hardly the same, is it, with a girl? I mean, I'm sorry for Caterina –"

"Sorry? Holy Heaven!"

"Nobody could possibly expect me to go through with the marriage after this. I mean, to take a bride that Taddeo has had his filthy paws on – I have to think of my family –"

Sandro's howl of indignation cut him short. "Mother of God! You talk as though Caterina were a clean shirt some one else had put on! She's a *person*, a human being, with ten times the character you'll ever have. Taddeo can't change that, whatever he does. He can't touch her heart and mind. She'll still be Caterina."

"You can't be expected to understand," said Roderigo stiffly. "The men of the Sorbolo family are rather particular about marrying virgins. The Spinellis would feel just the same. I know that her father will regard the betrothal contract as null and void."

Sandro took a deep breath. "And what," he asked, "is to happen to Caterina?"

"I should think the best thing would be if Taddeo married her."

"The *best* thing?" Sandro echoed incredulously. How

could any one keep calm when listening to such stark in-sensitive idiocy?

"I imagine that Spinelli will write and demand that he does just that."

"You have met Taddeo. Can you imagine any decent father wishing his daughter to marry a creature like that?"

"Beggars can't be choosers, can they? After what's hap-pened, Spinelli will be glad to find any husband he can for her."

"Thank you," said Sandro with heavy politeness. "I think we have nothing more to say to each other." He stalked out. His hands were trembling.

CHAPTER FIFTEEN

Castel Sismondo

"You must be mad," said Caterina as they rode down into the coastal lowlands.

Taddeo grinned. "So you keep telling me."

"Dragging me off like this! What can you hope to gain?"

"You," he said. "I always fancied you."

Inwardly terrified, she kept up an air of cool defiance. "I would sooner be dead than have anything to do with you. Especially after today."

"That makes it more interesting. Hunting or horse-breaking – or girls – if there's no difficulty there's no sport."

They rode in silence for a time. In the first few moments on the hilltop she had learned the hopelessness of trying to break away. The men hemmed her in. She could feel bruises coming up on her arms where they had gripped her.

"Where are you taking me?" she demanded at last.

"Rimini."

"But Malatesta threw you out!"

"That was the story." He laughed. "Don't worry, we are sure of our welcome, though my Lord Sigismondo won't be there to do the honours. His last message said he would be marching to the south."

"So – you've been in touch, working for him all the time?"

He nodded, pleased to have fooled every one.

She thought desperately. Hope of rescue had died in the first minutes. Her father could have done nothing with his few servants. Anyhow, he could never have overtaken them. In due time, of course . . . but she could not see beyond the approaching night. Her skin crept at the thought of Taddeo.

She closed her eyes and prayed fervently to her patron saint, that Santa Caterina, the virgin of Alexandria who in ancient days had been martyred on the wheel of spikes. Only a miracle would help her now.

But blind faith had never come easily to her. Her mind had been shaped too much by the old pagan writers, she was more at home in a world where clear-eyed men and women endured their fate with stoic courage, not calling on heedless gods.

She opened her eyes again. Rimini was nearer now. The towers of the new Castel Sismondo stood up against the pale background of the sea.

"You will not have to sleep in a monastery tonight," said Taddeo with a chuckle. "It looks grim from the outside but that is misleading. He's sparing no expense. It's quite luxurious."

"I would rather sleep in a ditch!"

"Well, I wouldn't." He began to hum under his breath.

She wondered suddenly if he still had the dagger he had stolen in Mantua. Not that it mattered, he had one at his belt. She remembered reading in Latin of the virtuous Lucretia who had stabbed herself after being raped by Tarquin. She and Margherita had agreed afterwards that Lucretia, if she had been sensible, would have stabbed Tarquin instead. In any case, Christians weren't allowed

144

to commit suicide. Self-defence was different. She shuddered. If . . . if she could get her fingers round the handle of a dagger when she was alone with Taddeo, could she steel herself to drive the blade into the soft flesh? She did not know. If the moment came, she would find out.

Another hour's riding brought them to the city. They clattered over the long drawbridge of the castle. The moat, cold grey in the spring afternoon, must be a hundred feet wide. The great towers, their new masonry smooth and light-coloured, rose almost the same distance against the scudding clouds.

"My Lord Sigismondo will be sorry to miss his new guest," said Taddeo. "Perhaps as well, though. He has too keen an eye for the girls himself. He might be *too* hospitable."

The sentries knew him and saluted. The party passed beneath the dangling portcullis in its shadowy tunnel and emerged into the first courtyard. It was crowded with horses and armed men. Laden baggage-animals were being marshalled into place. Clearly, some considerable party was about to leave.

"*No!*" Taddeo muttered furiously under his breath. "The devil!"

They all reined in, bunched for a moment awkwardly, with soldiers and servants milling round them. Then, from an inner courtyard, came a tall, wiry young man, splendid in cloth of gold. Caterina had never set eyes upon him before, but she knew it could be only one person, the legendary, the notorious Sigismondo Malatesta, Lord of Rimini.

Taddeo was out of his saddle in an instant, cap off, down on one knee on the paved yard. A hand, flashing with rings, was outstretched for him to kiss. She heard a silken voice. "I knew it – Taddeo! You have a talent for self-preservation."

"I – I thought my lord was in the south –"

"So I was. And now I am hurrying back there. You can ride a mile or two with me. I want to know about Urbino."

"By all means, my lord." Taddeo managed to inject delight and eagerness into his voice. He rose to his feet. Malatesta, glancing past him, became aware of Caterina, statue-still on her horse, Grifone wary at her elbow.

"I see you have not come back empty-handed, Taddeo. Who is this?"

She heard her own voice cutting across the buzz of the crowd, overtopping Taddeo's discreet murmur.

"I am Caterina Spinelli, my lord. I was brought here against my will. I appeal to you, my lord, as a man of honour –"

Malatesta strode forward. Taddeo, big as he was, seemed suddenly no more impressive than a mongrel at his heels. Caterina looked down from her saddle, forcing herself to meet those basilisk eyes, glittering from under the flat lids. Those were the days of the young Sigismondo, when he had the cruel beauty of a falcon. It would be many years yet before he was denounced by the Pope as a wife-murderer, "hated by God and man" for that and count-less other crimes, his effigy solemnly burnt on the steps of St Peter's. But even on that day in Rimini Caterina knew the irony of her own phrase. "Man of honour", indeed . . . Yet he represented her one slim hope of defence against Taddeo.

He returned her stare. A smile crinkled his lips. The brilliant eyes ran over her, down to the small foot resting in its stirrup. "You appeal to me?" he echoed. "Yes, you do indeed appeal to me." Over his shoulder, not taking his eyes off her, he tossed the words to Taddeo, like a bone to a dog, "Thank you, Taddeo. You have excellent taste." He snapped his fingers and some kind of majordomo appeared beside him, staff of office in hand. "See that this young lady is lodged comfortably until I come home again." This time he turned and spoke directly to Taddeo. "And when you have given me your report from Urbino, you will come back here and help to guard her."

"Yes, my lord." Taddeo all but choked on the words.

Malatesta tittered, relishing his own malice. "I shall hold you personally responsible for her safety." A page led forward his horse. He mounted, and wheeled towards Caterina. Now he loomed over her. The hooked nose increased the likeness to a predatory bird. "I regret that my military affairs call me away. We shall meet again. Oh, yes, we shall meet again."

The watchful trumpeters raised their instruments. The fanfare quivered in the air, the press of horsemen unwound into an orderly column. Malatesta vanished through the gateway, Taddeo trotting obsequiously behind. He had time only to send her one vicious glance of frustration.

Caterina saw that for the present there was nothing to be done. No one would dare to disobey Malatesta. She dismounted with dignity and allowed herself to be escorted through archways, up staircases, and along passages to one of the towers overlooking the moat. One more flight of steps, and she was bowed through a door into the quarters that were to form her own enclosed little world for the immediate future.

One or two small anterooms, a curtained recess in the outer wall, which must contain the usual privy, cupboard-doors with fine intarsia panelling, a bed for a servant . . . these preliminary details she took in as she passed by and entered the principal room. Everything was bright and fresh. The blue ceiling was powdered with silver stars. There was a great bed, draped in crimson. A serving man was already on his knees before a tall fireplace carved with a line of cupids. His torch kindled the brushwood, he laid slim pine-logs on the crackling flames. The resinous fragrance filled the room, the orange light danced up and down the plastered walls. They were newly frescoed, a series of scenes illustrating the amours of Jupiter. The pale figures almost came to life as she glanced. They seemed to writhe in the flickering glow.

She had not seen so splendid a room since Mantua. It was true then, what they said about Malatesta. He might be a monster of depravity, but his artistic taste could hardly be faulted. However, she was in no mood to appreciate it. Unsmiling, she took her stand in front of the fire, warming her hands. Servants bustled about behind her, she heard the crisp rustle of clean linen as the bed was made. A black slave-girl, a girl no older than herself, appeared silently at her elbow, offering a silver basin and a towel. The steam rising from the warm water came perfumed to her nostrils.

The majordomo coughed discreetly. He trusted the young lady would be comfortable. He appreciated that she had arrived without baggage or her own maid, but the black girl, Lucia, was well trained. She did not know much Italian, but it was quite easy to make her understand one's needs.

"This is a beautiful apartment," he said.

"It is a prison, though."

He laughed at that. "Madam should see our dungeons!" For all his fine manners, thought Caterina sourly, he is Malatesta's man. He bowed himself out. As he reached the doorway there was a muffled snarling in the distance,

148

the cold savagery of which startled her out of the aloofness she was striving to maintain.

"What was that?"

"My lord's leopards. It is about their feeding time. They are caged in the next tower. There is nothing to be afraid of."

"I'm not afraid of leopards," she said.

"But my Lord Sigismondo has not been here for the past two weeks," said the majordomo, "and he is not expected for another ten days."

We made sure of that, Sandro said to himself with dour satisfaction, or we should not have been such fools as to stick our noses under your gateway.

Aloud, he said nothing, remembering his pretended role as an underling. He stood in the background and left Marliano to do the talking.

The sly little Venetian was just the man for this job. It had been a stroke of luck, his travelling through Urbino at the right moment. Sandro had met him more than once in his father's shop and Marliano was delighted to oblige the son of his best customer in Mantua. "I want one night inside the castle at Rimini," Sandro had said. "Nothing easier," Marliano had promised with the assurance of one whose business took him into half the princely homes of Italy.

A book would form the best bait, a rare manuscript, rarely illustrated, since Malatesta's passion for culture was well known. It did not matter that Marliano's present stock contained no such book. It wasn't the first time, in forty years of glib selling, that Marliano had sung the merits of some item he did not possess. The manuscript would be "for my Lord Sigismondo's eyes alone". They must take care to arrive in Rimini when they were certain he was away, and late in the afternoon, so as to be offered overnight lodging before going on, as they would promise, to seek him in his camp. Marliano's responsibility would end there. He need know nothing, not risk his neck in the slightest. It was up to Sandro to use his time well and get news of Caterina.

He had to be prepared for running into Taddeo. But the Castel Sismondo, being still under construction, was known to be full of strangers coming and going – labourers, craftsmen, artists from distant places, some spending only a few days in the place while they carried out their particular commission. In such a crowd of constantly changing faces it should be easy to escape notice. Marliano, determined for his own sake to avoid being mixed up in any trouble, helped him to darken his hair still further and to stain his face and hands to a Sicilian swarthiness. A smooth stone, slipped into the right foot of his hose, did not trouble him when riding but gave him a marked limp – "nothing like a distinctive walk", said the Venetian, who was remarkedly well informed on the tricks of spies and criminals. Shabbily dressed, and humbly occupied in the midst of Marliano's half-dozen genuine servants, Sandro bore little resemblance to Federigo's debonair young paymaster.

It was almost too easy. The majordomo was obviously nervous lest any lack of attention on his part should prompt the merchant to carry his bargain to some rival collector. He was insistent that the party should sup and sleep at Rimini. With so many of the soldiers away on campaign there were plenty of empty quarters round the outer courtyard.

Sandro had to work fast. His chance came after supper. Returning an empty wine-jug to the butler, he managed to strike up a conversation with one of the serving girls.

He had marked her down as the plainest. He guessed she would be the readiest for a mild flirtation in the shadows outside the kitchen door. His compliments set her giggling agreeably. Hoping no doubt for further developments, she seemed more than willing to linger and gossip. After a few nonsensical exchanges he began cautiously to probe.

Oh, yes, there was a young gentleman named Taddeo Tregani . . . back now in my Lord Sigismondo's service after being away some time . . . Yes, she sniggered, you had to watch that one! He was in the castle at this moment. It was too funny, really—

"How, funny?" He tried to sound casual.

She explained. The young Lord Taddeo, as he liked to be called, had run off with a gentlewoman from San Stefano. (Sandro's nails dug into his palms as he listened.) He had brought her straight here to Rimini. But he had had the bad luck to run into my Lord Sigismondo just as he was leaving. My lord had seen the girl, liked her, and decreed that she be kept safe until his return. Poor Lord Taddeo had been made her jailer, responsible for her, but unable to lay a finger on her himself. Every one was laughing at the Lord Taddeo – only behind his back, because he could be a devil when he was angry.

"And this girl? She's still here?"

"She'd better be! Or when my Lord Sigismondo comes back, I can guess what he'll do to Taddeo."

The girl was shut up in one of the towers. One wasn't supposed to mention it, really. After all, the Lord Sigismondo had a wife, poor soul, and though she must know all about his behaviour with other women there was no cause to humiliate her any more. The servant hadn't herself set eyes on the beautiful captive. Her meals were fetched by a black slave-girl, who didn't say much because she knew very little Italian.

Sandro established that the tower in question was next to the menagerie – and *that* was easy to identify from the occasional roars and snarls which floated down to the courtyard. It was evident that the servant had told him all she knew. To pursue the question would only stir suspicion. He made himself dally with her for a little longer, then pretended that Marliano would be requiring his services, and soothed her evident disappointment with a shamelessly false promise to seek her out on the next evening.

He was limping away across the courtyard, returning her wistful "good-night" with a carefree answer, when a hand descended on his shoulder and spun him into the circle of light thrown by a torch bracketed to the wall.

"Well, I'm damned!" said Grifone merrily. "I thought the voice at least was familiar. My master will be interested." He dropped his own voice. "Don't try anything, please. I've got this dagger at your ribs."

CHAPTER SIXTEEN

Lucia

TADDEO had changed since their last encounter in Urbino. Sandro detected a new bitterness in his voice and etched more deeply on his face. There had always been something twisted about Taddeo, but it seemed as though recent events had given him an extra wrench.

He received Sandro in his own chamber. Grifone and another man planted themselves by the door.

"How did *you* get here?"

"It was easy – I slipped in with the crowd." Sandro was determined that Marliano should not suffer if he could help it. It would be hard to connect him with the merchant's party, unless there was a general interrogation throughout the castle. Long before then, Marliano should be safely away.

Taddeo surveyed his darkened hair and skin with malicious amusement. "So you've taken to disguises? My Lord Sigismondo does not like spies."

"I'm not here as a spy, you know that. Not in a military sense."

"We might find it hard to convince him. You're Federigo's man. And they're at war."

"Federigo did not send me. I'm here because of Caterina."

Taddeo winced. "*I* can't help you."

"You brought her here – against her will. You could let her go."

"To please *you*?"

"Oh, no. For an agreed sum in florins."

"Always the merchant's son!"

Sandro did not rise. Keeping his voice as pleasant and persuasive as he could, he said: "Even kings are not too proud to deal in ransoms." As Taddeo did not at once reply he continued: "If you're wondering what guarantee I can give you, you need not worry. The Spinellis can raise something. And Federigo will advance me the rest."

Taddeo found his voice. "Do you know what you're asking me? Do you know what Malatesta would do to me if he came back and found –"

"He need not find *you*, any more than Caterina. You can come with us to Urbino – I promise safe-conduct, in Federigo's name. Then you can go where you like. And you won't be empty-handed." Sandro searched his face eagerly. Surely he had made the right approach? Money was what Taddeo would understand?

Taddeo brooded. Sandro did not blame him for taking time. It was a big decision, a turning point. If Taddeo broke with Malatesta now he would cut short a profitable career at Rimini and gain a dangerous enemy. On the other hand, he could bargain for a sum probably bigger than he had ever handled before, and one which would enable him to set up as an independent condottiere anywhere else in Italy: also, he would enjoy his revenge on Malatesta.

He waited for Taddeo to ask, "How much?" but when the young Perugian spoke he said, surprisingly, "You would like to see Caterina?"

"Now?" Sandro's heart leapt. "Of course."

"Bind his hands with this cord, Grifone. It will look

154

more proper," said Taddeo sardonically, "if we meet any one as we go along the battlements."

The other soldier held a flaring torch to light their way. The night air had a tang of salt, but, as they filed along the ramparts, the sea smell gave place to the rank stench of the leopards.

"Caterina is lodged in the next tower. My Lord Sigismondo collects beautiful pets, four-footed and otherwise." Taddeo stopped and beckoned them through an open doorway. Inside, the atmosphere was overpowering. The man with the torch raised it. Fierce eyes, like jewels, flashed back the light. There were half a dozen cages ranged round the circumference of the tower. The great cats snarled and flung themselves against the iron bars. "They are particularly hungry now," Taddeo explained. "They are kept without food one day in seven – for their health, you know, to imitate their natural wild conditions. Today was their fast."

Sandro shuddered. Taddeo seemed in no hurry to move on. "Caterina –" he prompted. Taddeo seemed not to hear.

"Beautiful, aren't they? All those delicate markings. Like rosettes of black. On golden velvet."

"Yes, they are beautiful. But they look cruel."

"Oh, they are, they are. But isn't that a rather stimulating mixture? Isn't it just right for Malatesta?"

"You know more about him than I do." Taddeo still made no move. He stood in front of one swishing beast, a private smile on his lips. "You said that Caterina was in the next tower?"

Taddeo swung round. Sandro did not like the sudden change in his tone. "I think it is rather late to disturb her."

"But you offered –"

"I thought it might save an undignified struggle."
Taddeo's features were suddenly contorted in the red
torch-light. "Did you really imagine you could buy me?"

"Then what are we doing up here?"

"You have to be put somewhere out of harm's way. I
thought a leopard-cage would be rather amusing."

"You don't mean you'd –"

"Hush! You don't know, Sandro, what pleasure it
gives me – at last – to see you really paralysed with fear.
No, I'm not going to push you in with the animals. It
would be all over in moments, and I've waited far too
long for the chance to pay you out. I've another idea.
Grifone, there's an empty cage over there. Unbolt it, will
you?"

Caterina had seen little of Taddeo during those two weeks
at Rimini.

He visited her on the first morning to inquire in a cold,
impersonal way whether she had everything she required.
The black slave-girl had already, with scarcely a word
spoken between them, supplied her needs. That was lucky:
she would have disliked begging for handkerchiefs and a
change of underclothes. Only on his next visit, two days
later, did boredom drive her to ask for something to read.
Books were brought her from the castle library, hand-
somely bound and bearing Malatesta's emblem, the
elephant's head. Taddeo had chosen Ovid, Petrarch,
Boccaccio and a collection of insipid verses by the tame
poets Malatesta liked to gather at his court.

She sat for hours, reading or just brooding, in the
alcoved window of her room. It faced seawards to the
sunrise. There was little to be seen but the vast expanse
of water below, rippling like silk, changing its colour
through the long day, silver to blue to grey to gold to

crimson, responsive to the sky. Gulls mocked her with their casual swoops of freedom. An occasional ship, lurching under its painted sails, was a rare distraction, especially if it swung round to enter the harbour of Rimini. Most craft crept by in the middle distance, bound for Venice or some southern port.

Mornings and evenings she was allowed exercise. She could make the circuit of the ramparts while Lucia tidied her room. These were the sole occasions when she could look inland, wistfully, to the piled-up mountains of the Marches, hiding her home amid their folds. She was not encouraged to linger in public view, though she might stand under cover, by the leopard-cages, and watch the raw meat poked to them through the bars.

At first Taddeo himself supervised these excursions. His strange withdrawn manner persisted. She realised that he was under strain. She could not believe that he had ever "loved" her in any sense deserving the use of that word, but – to her own misfortune – she had stirred his desire. He had had her in his grasp, and then been forced to drop her, like one of those leopards sulkily surrendering at a growl from a larger beast. Not an elegant comparison, especially for herself, she reflected acidly, but it sprang all too readily to mind as she watched them squabbling over the dark red flesh.

Hungry leopards soon forgot their resentment, frustrated men remembered longer. She understood Taddeo's feelings when, as they passed soldiers on the ramparts, she caught the men's sly smiles. Taddeo's humiliation was common knowledge. Small wonder that he no longer enjoyed the company he had once sought, which now only tantalised him and advertised his discomfiture. After the first week, he sent Grifone to do duty in his place.

There were these brief interludes and occasional visits

from a servant with a basket of logs or a pail of water. Otherwise, Caterina's human contacts were limited to the almost wordless companionship of Lucia.

In the first days she viewed the African girl with distrust. It was not only her blackness and her silent flitting movements that suggested a shadow: it was because she was almost always there, inescapable. Clearly she had been set to watch Caterina, and watch her she did, with those enigmatic eyes, like some wild creature patient in its woodland ambush, ready to pounce. It was uncanny and disturbing. Caterina was thankful when the slave turned the key in the outer door and left her alone. And that precaution was unnecessary, Caterina told herself. If she had managed to get out unguarded, she would have been challenged before she was half-way to the gates. At night she might have reached the gates but they would be shut anyhow.

It was all hopeless. She paced her room, stared at the empty sea, tried to find mental escape – at least – in the books allowed to her. But one could not read all day, one could not evade thought about the future. Any day Malatesta might be back in Rimini.

Gradually her feelings towards her black jailer underwent a change. It was impossible to be cooped up with one person, day after day, and have no feelings. Whatever her orders to observe the captive and if necessary spy on her – and Caterina took such instructions for granted – Lucia contrived to convey an unspoken goodwill, a consideration expressed in the simplest attentions. The way in which she set out the meal, turned down the bed-sheet, or wrapped the towel round Caterina's shoulders as she stepped dripping from the wooden bathtub – it was something a little more than the service of a well-trained maid. Rather were the routine actions like signals of sympathy.

"I wish I could talk to her!" Caterina once muttered fervently when the isolation of her room threatened to become unbearable.

Lucia's rare smile flashed whitely. "Madam wishes conversation?"

Caterina stared. "The majordomo said you did not speak Italian!"

"Not like a Florentine, madam." The girl laughed modestly. It was as though a window between them had suddenly been unshuttered. "But always I listen. I try to improve."

"You speak well. And I thought you knew only a few words. Why on earth didn't you tell me?"

The smile faded. "At first I thought you were like all the others."

"Others?"

"Masters and mistresses." She shrugged. "They wish us just to understand orders, no more. They do not want to share thoughts. To them we are not people. Often it is better not to let them know how much we understand."

"And how do you know I am different?"

"I feel – here." Lucia laid a dark hand between her breasts. "Also, you are not free. You too."

"How do you come to be in Rimini?"

"Ah, a long story."

"We are not short of time here," said Caterina. She made a face and the black girl laughed responsively.

Lucia had come, like most foreign slaves, through the market at Venice. Before that, there had been a ship from Cyprus. And before that she had muddled childhood memories of many places. First the wilderness, so hot, so green. Then Antioch, Damascus, Damietta . . . the names came hesitantly. Famagusta she would never forget. It was in Famagusta she had been taken from her mother.

Caterina said hastily, "And at last you came to Rimini?"

Lucia nodded. "A Venetian senator bought me as a present for the Lord Sigismondo. It was meant as a joke, I think . . ." Her tone was bitter. "A joke between great gentlemen."

"Why?"

"I heard the Venetian laugh with his friends. I heard him say, 'Malatesta likes girls of all shapes and sizes and colours – I wonder what he will make of this one.' But when I came –"

"Yes?" Caterina listened with horrified fascination.

"He was in a bad mood. He said –" Lucia's voice faltered. "He said, they might as well have sent him an ape."

Caterina's hand went out instinctively. It was the first conscious physical contact she had made with the girl, though Lucia had brushed her hair and helped her into her dresses.

"*I* think you're beautiful," she said simply.

She meant it. She had been thinking earlier, studying Lucia's face and figure before there was the bond of speech between them, that the girl was like a breathing statue, cast in dark bronze. Cheekbone and temple gleamed with an almost metallic sheen.

"Yes, beautiful," she repeated. "But I'm glad Malaesta didn't think so. Aren't you?"

"Now, yes. But at the time, when he laughed in his anger, and pushed me away, I was –"

"Humiliated?"

"Humiliated." Lucia accepted the word with a grateful nod. "Humiliated," she repeated thoughtfully. "That word, in Italian, I should know."

So began what Caterina realised was the first real friendship she had shared with another girl since the happy days with Margherita Gonzaga. Lucia opened like a blossom in the first warmth of spring. She had a gurgling humour, a darting intelligence, which she at last felt free to display. No one, she explained, since she had been snatched away from her family in the Famagusta slave-market, had ever treated her as a person. She had been a property, an investment, a useful household thing, or, at the most, a pet. Never a human individual.

"But with you," she told Caterina, "at last I feel that I can stand upright –" She squared her shoulders and tossed back her turbaned head. "On two feet," she said, as if defying the world.

They talked of many things in those long days together, above all of themselves. Lucia too faced a grey future. If, by some miracle, she were to be given her freedom, there could be no going home. She did not know where "home" had been. She had no kindred she could ever hope to find again. Italy she liked well enough. She could have been happy here in different circumstances. "If only we were at my home in San Stefano," said Caterina wistfully, "your circumstances would be very different, I promise you!"

Their friendship, like Lucia's command of Italian, was a secret best kept between them. When other people came to their quarters, Lucia instantly became the enigmatic wordless attendant again. But Caterina, confident now of her goodwill, began to entertain wild hopes of something more. If only a means could be found, might not Lucia help her to escape?

Promenading the ramparts, morning and evening, however, she got little comfort from her study of the fortress. She felt dizzy when she craned over the battlements and saw the water so far below. More than ever she admired Sandro for his part in the recapture of San Stefano.

Continuing her walk, she eyed the gatehouse and the long causeway, with its drawbridge, spanning the wide moat. To pass the gates would need a most convincing disguise. Disguises for two, indeed. No plan was feasible unless it included Lucia's escape as well. The girl must be made to see that. She should have her freedom, she should have an honoured position in the household at San Stefano or be at liberty to go wherever she wished, but she could not possibly stay here to face Malatesta's fury, even if she survived Taddeo's. His alone, Caterina felt certain, would be vicious enough.

The more she considered, the more the difficulties multiplied. Suppose, she thought dispiritedly – suppose we got out of the castle, in God knows what disguise, for what could Lucia become except perhaps a black *boy*, and she had already said that, alas, there were none in the whole Malatesta household? Yet – suppose us on the far side of that moat, strolling unchallenged into the distance – where do we head for, how far can we get? She herself knew only that San Stefano lay somewhere behind that crinkled skyline to the south-west. Lucia would know nothing. Once out of Rimini all the responsibility would be her own. How could she ask Lucia to join in such a suicidal venture? Lucia, after all, was facing no particular fresh afflictions if she remained an obedient slave and carried out her orders. It was only Caterina who was desperate to escape – yet no escape could be imagined in which Lucia did not take part.

Caterina's thoughts went round and round hopelessly. It was an unbroken circle, like the ramparts of the Castel Sismondo itself. No way out.

She was beginning the third week of her captivity when, to her surprise, Taddeo appeared in person to escort her on her morning exercise. He wore an air of suppressed excitement. His eyes were wild. Her first thought, in her innocence, was that he might be starting a bout of the marsh fever so many of the boys had suffered from at Mantua.

Usually they turned left and walked round the battlements clockwise. This morning he caught her arm roughly – he had never touched her since their arrival in Rimini – and seemed anxious to go the other way. She shrugged. What did it matter? One reached the same destination at the end of the walk. One got – nowhere. She turned with him towards the leopard tower.

"Something to show you." The cold, self-controlled correctness of his recent behaviour was gone. He was pleased with himself, sniggering almost.

"Oh?" she said distantly. "What?"

"You'll see. A rather splendid addition to the menagerie."

She assumed they would turn into the doorway, but he put out an arm and steered her past. They continued round the open sentry-walk and then, a few paces beyond the tower, he stopped and looked down at her with a self-conscious smile.

"Well?" she said.

The paved walk stretched empty before them in the morning sun. She could see nothing at all unusual. But still he waited, wearing that odd, almost insane grin.

"That rope – ?" she began doubtfully.

She had noticed some thick rope, wound many times round one of the merlons, and tightly secured. It must be something to do with the workmen. Somewhere or other in the castle building operations were in progress the whole time.

"Take a look," he invited her. "No – you will see

better from here." He drew her some paces further along the battlements and she obediently leant over.

Suspended at the end of the rope, dangling in mid-air perhaps ten feet below the ramparts, was one of the leopard-cages. From where she stood, she had a slanting view and could see through the bars. As the cage spun dizzily in the glare of the sun she noticed a huddled figure inside. Not a leopard, but a man.

Taddeo was pressing against her in the embrasure of the battlements. "Go on," he whispered. "Say good-morning to your beloved Sandro!"

CHAPTER SEVENTEEN

The Cage

SANDRO's real ordeal had begun only an hour or two before Caterina's distracted cry reached him from the wall above.

When, late the previous evening, Taddeo's men had untied his wrists and thrust him into the empty cage, he had assumed that it was just a characteristic act of malice on Taddeo's part. He must be locked up somewhere overnight. To put him in a cage instead of a cell, and leave him with restless, growling beasts as neighbours, was the kind of idea to tickle the Perugian's perverted sense of humour. He did not take in the meaning of Taddeo's murmured remark to Grifone, "This will do for tonight. We shall need to see what we are doing."

The night was long, chilly and unpleasant. Probably he could not have slept anyhow in such discomfort and with such anxieties revolving in his brain. The proximity of the leopards put sleep out of the question. So the hours dragged by till dawn. No one came near him, though on several occasions he heard a sentry's tread outside.

Dawn brought Grifone with a cup of red wine and a hunk of bread. "Quick, sir." He held them to the bars for Sandro to take. "Not supposed to do this." He appeared embarrassed. In the early light streaming greyly through the door, his scarred features had lost their usual roguishness. "God's my witness," he said hoarsely, "if I'd known he'd think of a trick like this, I'd never have –"

"You did your duty." Sandro drained the cup and passed it back. He felt better after the wine. He still thought Grifone was apologising for his ignominious imprisonment. The soldier looked as if he were about to say more, but the words would not come. He stared at the empty cup in his hand and took it as an excuse to go. He left with a guilty haste which Sandro put down to his disobedience in supplying the breakfast.

The true reason became apparent when Taddeo arrived an hour later. At his heels tramped several men whom Sandro recognised as his attendants in Urbino, though Grifone was not among them, and in the rear came a number of burly workmen.

"Wheel it out," Taddeo ordered.

The workmen pushed and pulled. On squeaking wheels, which threw the leopards into a frenzy of indignation, Sandro's cage was eased through the archway into the glare of the newly risen sun.

"What *are* you doing?" demanded Sandro with as much dignity as he could put on. It was not easy to be dignified when you were being trundled along and had to snatch at the bars to keep your balance.

"Animals do not talk," said Taddeo pleasantly.

Workmen were passing thick ropes round the cage. One had climbed on to the roof. His feet scraped overhead, and there was the dull thump of slack rope falling on the wood. Other men were fitting up a contraption of beams and pulley against the battlements. He could not see clearly, but it looked like one of the cranes the builders used for hoisting blocks of stone.

A ghastly suspicion seized him. He remembered the cage, high on the tower at Mantua. The criminal slowly dying. No . . . Taddeo would not do this to him, not even Taddeo –

The cage lurched under him, rose unsteadily a few inches off the flagstones, spun a quarter circle, spun back. "Whoa!" shouted a man. His voice was matter-of-fact. It might have been an ordinary building operation.

"All right," said Taddeo.

Sandro knew then that Taddeo would.

He let out a choking gasp of horror. Afterwards he hoped it had gone unheard amid the general babble. Certainly it went unheeded.

It was futile to cry out. Pleas for mercy would only have increased Taddeo's perverted pleasure. He fought down the hysteria that welled up inside him as the cage rose jerkily above the ring of uptilted faces and then swung sideways over the battlements.

For a few moments he could look down on them all. Some, like Taddeo, grinned up at him with the brutish glee of cruel children. Some stared wide-eyed with a terrible shame-faced fascination. Others turned deliberately away. One old workman made the sign of the cross.

Then those who were leaning back on the rope began to pass it inch by inch through their fingers. The cage sank slowly. He was level with the embrasures, he was below them, he now faced blank masonry, only by pressing his cheek hard against the cold bars, and screwing his eyes upwards into the sun's glare, could he see the top of the wall. The cage stopped. It spun a little, till one corner bumped the stonework, and it spun the other way. Gradually it settled into an uncertain stillness, immediately disturbed when he moved.

He moved now, so that he could not be seen by Taddeo, who was peering over to mock him with a tirade of obscene insults, like someone demented. He looked outwards through the bars and recoiled with a shudder from what he saw: the sea, infinitely remote below him, and the tawny beach marching northwards into the hazy distance. Vertigo swept over him. He closed his eyes.

From the battlements Taddeo was screaming, like the voice of Doom. "And you can stay there till you rot!"

"God have mercy on me," Sandro muttered.

Caterina could only echo that prayer when she looked down and saw.

She turned and implored Taddeo to release him. At that moment she would have done anything Taddeo wanted. But she saw from the conflict in his face that no bargain was possible. Taddeo was too frightened of Malatesta. It was only with Sandro that he was free to do as he liked. In tormenting Sandro he found release for his thwarted emotion.

What comfort could she call down to the prisoner in the cage? She was too frantic to think coherently. The whole situation was one of unimaginable horror, and she had walked into it without the slightest warning. She did not even grasp, till she thought it over in her room afterwards, that Sandro's presence in Rimini was linked with her own. At first she supposed he had been taken prisoner in battle. Only when she recalled some of Taddeo's words did she begin to realise the special significance of this macabre encounter he had staged on the battlements.

She shouted something, she never remembered clearly what useless, feeble phrases came to her lips. But never, for the rest of her life, did she forget the answer from the cage. Sandro's voice was steady. At that time he had been there only an hour or so, long enough to overcome his first panic, but not to be weakened by the hunger and thirst and exposure that were to follow.

"Don't cry," he told her. "That's what Taddeo wants. I'm prepared for anything now. Caterina – are you still there?"

"Yes!"

"I'm trying to remember that passage old Vittorino made us learn – where Socrates is sentenced to death and tells the jury he doesn't care." He began to quote the Greek *"There is much reason to hope that death is a good thing. For either death is a state of nothingness and utter unconsciousness, or, as men say* – Can you remember how it goes on?"

"I – I think so." Her mind flew back to the schoolroom at Mantua. Fighting to keep the tears out of her voice she continued the Greek, *"or, as men say, there is a change and a migration of the soul from this world to another."*

"Yes," he said. "So – either way – Socrates said there was nothing to fear."

At this point Taddeo, finding no amusement in their conversation, hustled her back to her own place of captivity. There, alone except for Lucia, she collapsed on the bed and let the tears flow.

For a long time the black girl made only soothing murmurs and stroked her head. When at last Caterina sat up and said chokily, "If only there was something I could do!" Lucia answered quietly, "We must think. Already I am thinking."

Caterina stared at her through misted eyes, then wiped them with the handkerchief Lucia pressed between her fingers. "You?"

"Why not? God did not make men to be treated like animals. Do you think that *I* do not feel that?" Lucia spoke with unusual intensity.

Caterina took her hand. "But what can we possibly do to save him?"

"I am thinking. It is very hard. He is young and strong, so he will not die quickly. Tonight he will still be alive – perhaps for several nights afterwards –"

"Oh, Lucia!" At these calculations Caterina nearly dissolved again into helpless sobbing. The black girl returned the pressure of her hand, which steadied her.

"At night there is no one on the battlements. The sentries pass only once each hour."

"What use is that? We could not pull up that heavy cage."

"No need. If the young man keeps his strength and nerve. Yes, I am thinking it must be tonight. After a second day without food and drink he will be too weak."

"What are you thinking of?" Caterina was herself again, intent and self-controlled.

"If he had a thing to –" Lucia's Italian for once became inadequate. "To cut –" She mimed.

"A file?"

"He opens the cage –"

"But –"

"Yes, it is terrible, down there. To open the door – and then nothing outside! But he is brave –"

"Oh, he *is*."

"And it is more terrible to stay in the cage until he dies. So – very carefully – he climbs on to the roof. I have been to look. The ropes go round it. There is plenty to hold."

"And to climb! Sandro could easily do that. In the ordinary way." Caterina felt a qualm of doubt. "If only he isn't too exhausted by then."

"I am saying, it must be tonight."

"It isn't very far to the top of the wall –"

"And I shall be there to help him."

"*You* will?"

Lucia smiled. "Of course. Some one must first climb down the rope and hand him the – the file?"

"I could do that!"

"Better for me." Again the white teeth flashed. "As a little child I climb many ropes and trees. I think, more than you."

Caterina did not argue. She looked at Lucia with increasing respect. It was like listening to Margherita in the old days. Lucia had an answer to everything.

But had she? How were they to get a file? "I find," Lucia promised brightly. "Everywhere in this place there are men working. And tools."

Caterina dared at last to indulge herself in a vision of Sandro free on the battlements. But – "free"? Even then he would be no more free than she was. And what would happen when the search started? Suspicion would fall quickly upon herself, and then equally upon Lucia. The plan was no use unless all three of them could escape from the castle.

That brought her back to the same old problem. She had gone over it until she was sick. Sandro's arrival made it even more insoluble. Three of them to pass the gates, now . . . and the alarm would have been given by then, the guards would check everybody.

She raised this difficulty. Lucia nodded gravely. "But I am not thinking of the gates. Can you –" Again the Italian word eluded her. She made sweeping movements with her arms.

"Yes, I can swim." Thank God for Mantua, the warm lagoon, the friendly help of the Gonzaga sisters! She could never have learned in the steep, boulder-strewn torrents round San Stefano.

The moat itself then presented no problem. But how to get down to it? The rope from which the cage hung had a considerable surplus length which had been wound repeatedly round one of the square merlons. If, having got Sandro safely out of the cage, they could lower it without a noise, would the rope reach to the water level, or near enough? It might wreck everything if they miscalculated. Perhaps, when she was taken for her evening exercise, she could observe how many times the rope encircled the merlon, and so arrive at a rough estimate of its length.

It was dreadfully risky, she thought. And even if the rope proved long enough, it was a severe physical test. She told herself that she could manage it – desperation must give her courage. She assumed that Lucia could face it. But what sort of condition would Sandro be in?

She remembered what he had told her about the San Stefano affair. How the old campaigners had taken his innocent proposal to do it by rope-climbing. "If only *we* had ladders," she said aloud.

"Ladders? Ah!"

"Oh, I know the castle is full of ladders. I've seen plenty in the far courtyard where the scaffolding is. But they might as well be a hundred miles away."

"We could never move those ladders," Lucia agreed. "I am thinking," she added. After a pause she said: "I look when I go to fetch the dinner."

"Look?"

"You see. Perhaps it is no good. I look."

She went out, bolting the outer door. So long as Caterina was left safely shut inside her quarters, Lucia was free to come and go on whatever domestic duties had to be done. After a longer absence than usual she returned with Caterina's meal, and then vanished again, leaving her to eat it. Caterina ate sparingly, putting aside some bread and a piece of meat which, if they could reach Sandro at all, he would be able to eat from his fingers. She had just put the food out of sight when the bolt slid back and Lucia entered. She was carrying what looked like a large bundle of clean bed-linen.

"You see. Ladders!"

She folded back the linen. The inside of the bundle was a mass of cordage, which, sorted out, was revealed as three rope-ladders. Caterina exclaimed with delight.

"Sometimes the workmen –" the black girl explained.

"Of course!"

For certain brief jobs, repairs and the like, it was easier for the workmen to let themselves down from the top of a wall than to set up heavy ladders from below. Thin as the cord was, Lucia had had a considerable burden to carry, but she made light of it. "I am used to burdens," she said. "This was more difficult to take." She drew a file from the bosom of her dress. She laughed. "These men are fussy about their tools."

Caterina was not satisfied until they had unrolled one ladder. She saw at once that the three, joined together would reach the water. She stowed them away quickly behind her bed. Short of some unusual alarm, and a search of her room, they were safe from discovery.

So, they had the file for the cage-bars, food for Sandro – she would save more at supper – and a way down from the battlements . . . There remained only the problem of clothes. All along, she had thought of possible escapes in male disguise. Now it seemed doubly desirable, if they had to negotiate rope-ladders and swim the moat.

Lucia looked down at her own voluminous gown and then at Caterina's. She grinned. "Yes! As a small girl in the hot forest I did not wear all this. No worry. In a great castle like this, quite easy. Everywhere page-boys. Everywhere they throw down their clothes. All the time asking, 'where is this? where is that?' Later, in the evening time, I look. You see."

And in due course Caterina saw.

173

CHAPTER EIGHTEEN

A Question of Life and Death

IF IT was a long day for Caterina it seemed even longer for Sandro.

The hours crawled. The strengthening sun beat into the cage and on to the wall behind, so that the heat came back at him from the baked stonework. Spring had rushed over the land in recent days, and down here on the coast much earlier than on the uplands. He took off his doublet. Even so, he sweated and longed for water.

He moved to a corner where there was a precious triangle of shade. The cage tilted under his weight. He felt a thrill of instinctive fear, then could have laughed at his own nervousness. For the one thing he could not possibly do was fall out of the cage. He rattled the sliding door. It would not budge. The simple latch which was enough to confine leopards had been reinforced, for his benefit, with a lock and chain.

Taddeo meant to spin out this business to the end. He was not going to let the victim shorten it, even when he went mad with thirst, by taking a suicidal leap.

Sandro thought a good deal about death during those hours. It was something very near, and coming inexorably nearer. He supposed that old people must spend much of their time facing the same fact, and, to judge from those he had known, it did not seem to disturb their serenity. It must be different, though, when you had a long life behind you. Different, too, when you might fairly hope for a gentle death, creeping upon you like sleep, welcome after tiredness and pain. And a death which, though it might well come tonight, would perhaps delay until next month, next year, even the year after.

To die young, in this cage, alone and without hope or comfort, was a sterner business. Yet, when the time was over – the ravening pangs first, he imagined, then the delirium and the weakness, until the slowing heart was stilled – it would be the same for him as for every man and woman who had gone before him to the grave. What? The Church promised resurrection and life. Plato and Socrates had been uncertain. Either life in a new world, they thought, or else oblivion. They had debated the alternatives with Master Vittorino – what had they *not* debated in those lively days at the Happy House? They had horrified that prim girl, Anna, by even considering that a pagan philosopher might be right and the priests wrong. It had been heady, dangerous talk, but at Mantua they had been afraid of nothing. And to boys and girls in a school-room death had seemed infinitely remote from themselves.

Well, he would know soon enough. Or rather, if the priests were mistaken and it was going to be oblivion, he would not know. And that would not matter. He would have gone like a snuffed candle.

But if the priests were right, how like Taddeo to lower him from the wall without giving him a chance to confess his sins and receive absolution! Even a condemned criminal was allowed that. Sandro ran over the events of the past few days. He had been to confession before starting out upon this disastrous venture. Since then, unless his feelings for Caterina were sinful, and the deceptions he had adopted to attempt her rescue, he could not accuse himself of any fresh wickedness. Still, it was inhuman of Taddeo not to have brought him a priest.

So the day passed. Mercifully the sun shifted. The shadow of the wall slanted across the cage. Far below, on the margin of the moat, he saw townspeople strolling like little coloured mannikins. They stopped and stared upwards. Word had got around, evidently. They could not restrain their curiosity. Sometimes their arms moved. Thin voices came up to him. He could not distinguish the words, he could not tell even whether they were jeering or shouting sympathy. He felt thankful that this side of the castle did not look over the town. That would have meant more idle people gaping up throughout the day. He preferred to be alone.

Several times Taddeo came to the battlements and hailed him. He would not give Taddeo the satisfaction of an answer. Let him rave, let him dredge the cesspit of his mind for ever fouler taunts. Taddeo himself shouted, in a way, like a spirit in torment. There was justice in that.

In the cool of the evening he heard Caterina's voice. He answered. "Is Taddeo with you?"

"No. I told him I would not come if he did. There are two soldiers instead. This is my time for exercise."

"It's – it's difficult to talk, Caterina."

"I know." Her voice was strained. It was probably emotion. Or the effort of projecting her voice from the battlements overhead. But was she trying to convey some double meaning, hidden from the guards, when she continued, "Tomorrow it may be easier."

"Tomorrow," he called back grimly, "I may not be here."

"That is true," she answered in a strangely neutral tone.

"I am still finding comfort in Plato. If we don't have the chance to talk again, think of the last words of Socrates when they led him from the court." He recited the Greek words that had kept on recurring to his mind throughout the day: "*The hour of departure has arrived, and we go our ways – I to die, and you to live. Which is better, only God knows.*"

"Oh, Sandro!" He was afraid she was going to break down. But she recovered herself. "I have another quotation from Plato that may give you comfort."

"What is it?"

"*Do not lose heart . . .*" She seemed to be fumbling for the Greek, as though the quotation did not come instantly to mind. Then, with a thrill of excitement, he realised that she was speaking words that Plato had never written. "*God willing, we shall set you free to-night.*"

"Say that again," he begged, incredulously.

She did so, this time more fluently.

"You are right," he called up to her. "Those ancient Greeks had some splendid thoughts."

For form's sake they talked for a little longer. Then, putting on a show of despair and sympathy to deceive her escort, they said good-night. The voices and footsteps died away.

What could she do, he wondered? She had said "we", so she must have accomplices. Caterina would not be so cruel as to offer him impossible hopes. He could do nothing but wait. At least he had something else to wait for now besides the certainty of death.

It was bitterly cold in the cage. Earlier he had been grilled by the sun. Darkness brought back a sharpness to the air. There was no moon. The sky was a rich fabric, sewn with tiny gem-sharp stars. Below him he could distinguish the dim shimmer of the moat and, farther off, the sea.

The night was silent except for the occasional creak of the ropes as the cage swung. At this level below the ramparts he was cut off from the myriad noises of the castle. Nothing penetrated to him but the footfalls of the sentry at long intervals, and, even more rarely, a surge of growling and snarling from the leopards. He could tell when the sentry halted to crane over the wall. Once the man shouted some ribald joke. He did not answer. At other times the sentries seemed only to pause, and then continue on their beat without disturbing him.

He knew he must be patient. Whatever was planned would be left until the rest of the castle was asleep.

Once more the heavy, deliberate footsteps . . . the slackening pace, the halt somewhere just above him, the ring of metal on pavement as the butt of the halberd came down . . . then the resumed patrol, the tread fading beyond the bulge of the next tower . . . This was the fifth time since darkness . . . Four hours, he speculated?

A few minutes passed. Then he was startled by something that swished past the end of the cage. An owl? A bat? He moved on all fours and stared through the bars. He could see nothing but the black mass of the wall, the glimmer of water far below, the pin-point stars above. All was silent again.

The cage creaked and swung. He put that down to his own scrambling movement across the floor. But, no, there was the slightest of bumps on the roof, as though some weight had been ever so cautiously dropped upon it. Then, from near the roof, a voice breathed rather than spoke through the bars.

"Sir?"

"Yes?" He kept his answer just as low.

A hand swooped down, discernible against the stars. A faint clink of glass on iron guided his own grasping fingers. "Do not drop," pleaded the voice. "Water." With trembling eagerness he wrapped his fingers round the little flagon, drew it through the bars, whipped out the stopper, and gulped at the contents.

The voice came again. A strange voice. It sounded like a girl's, but it was not Caterina's. The accent was foreign. Whoever it was must be lying on the top of the cage. And whoever it was must be brave, and very cool.

"Take this." A small tool was poked into his hand. "You must cut the bar. To open the door."

"Here?" he whispered stupidly. "You are not going to hoist me up?"

"We cannot. It is not possible for two girls."

"Caterina –?"

"She waits. Up there. Quickly, sir. We must not talk."

He took the file and ran his other hand over the fastening of the gate. He remembered it from his daylight investigation. The locked chain passed round the first bar of the sliding gate and the adjoining bar in the side of the cage. He had only to cut through the first bar and the chain would be freed. He began near the floor. It might be necessary to file through the bar higher up as well, removing a section, but perhaps he had strength to lever it aside sufficiently to release the chain after a single cut. He worked feverishly. The file made a considerable noise in the stillness, but that could not be helped. From down here it would scarcely carry into the castle, and it would be a long time before the sentry passed this way again. Obviously his rescuers had reckoned on that.

When he paused to rest, the voice asked anxiously: "You are all right? You have strength, sir? If not, I have food here, but –"

"No," he forced himself to answer. "I'll get out of here first."

The bar was cut through. He slipped the file into his doublet, took the bar in both hands, and strained at it. The veins stood out on his forehead. The bar yielded ever so slightly. He took a deep breath and exerted all his strength. There was a gap now where he had filed it. He pulled at the chain, forced it through the gap.

"Right," he panted.

"This will be the worst, sir. But slowly, and you cannot fall. I am helping."

"I can manage."

There was now only the ordinary latch. He lifted it and slowly slid back the cage-door. A square of sky appeared, unlined with bars. He felt suddenly nauseated at the thought of the drop, the emptiness, where the floor of his prison ended. He had got to go through there somehow – backwards, leaning outwards into the void, and clamber on to the top of the cage.

It was not a pleasant thought. But there was someone else lying perilously on the roof already, a stranger, a girl by the sound of her, risking her life for him. If *she* could do that . . .

"I am coming," he said between his teeth. With a silent prayer he edged head and shoulders through the open door and stretched an arm over the top of the cage. A warm hand guided his fingers till they closed on the rope where it ran round the cage. Another hand, reassuringly firm, was under his armpit.

He took one foot off the tilting floor, then the other. He heaved himself upwards. The shadowy stranger pulled, and continued to hold him tight. The cage swung violently under their exertions, but settled down again.

It was a girl kneeling beside him, though she wore

doublet and hose. She gave him time to recover his breath, but not to start thinking too much about their nightmare position.

"Now – only to climb, sir. You have strength?"

"Yes."

"It is not far."

She helped him to stand upright. They stood, feet apart, bracing themselves on the top of the cage, their hands on the rope. She looked up at him, her eyes white in her dark face. She motioned him to go first and he obeyed without argument. As he struggled upwards he felt her hand under the sole of his boot. It was strangely comforting. In the ordinary way the brief climb would have been nothing. Now he was weak and almost light-headed from his long ordeal. It took all his determination to reach the top.

There another hand reached for him. He heard Caterina's little sob of thankfulness as she helped him over the battlements. For a few moments they clung to each other. Then the other girl dropped silently to the paving at their side.

He had had little time to worry about the next step, how these two – seemingly without accomplices – were going to complete the escape. But their decisive manner suggested that they had it all worked out.

A torch, burning somewhere on the far side of the menagerie tower, diffused a pale pink radiance, but it merely threw the spot where they were standing into blacker shadow. As Caterina stepped back, he could just make out that she too was wearing a boy's tunic and hose. She drew him to the next embrasure. "We've a rope-ladder," she whispered. So that explained the swishing sound which had mystified him. "You'll find it much easier. Then there's only the moat."

"I shall be all right." He felt the cord. It was thin,

but presumably tough. "We'd better not all be on it at once."

"I'll go first then. I can help you in the water."

She disappeared over the wall. The cord tautened round the merlon. There were little twitching noises, mouse-like, against the stonework. He stood with the other girl, Lucia, at his side. Neither spoke. The night was so still, the very stars seemed to be listening.

Suddenly the silence was broken. He heard Taddeo's voice in the distance, raucous, thickened with wine. From an archway at the far corner, three towers along the ramparts from the menagerie, several figures lurched into the pool of light cast by one of the torches bracketed at intervals around the walls.

"Quick," he said roughly. He pushed Lucia towards the ladder.

"But –"

"You next," he insisted. She went.

He could hear the men coming noisily towards him, though now they were masked from view by one of the intervening towers. Taddeo was shouting something about a two-legged animal in a cage. Obviously they had been drinking late and were coming to amuse themselves at Sandro's expense.

He had to think quickly. Even if he went now, before Lucia was safely off the ladder, Taddeo might grasp what was happening in time to cut the rope. It wouldn't mean just a drop into the water, either. The wall splayed out at the base. Any one falling would strike a sloping plinth of masonry before rebounding into the moat.

Anyhow, the alarm mustn't be given yet. They must get clear into open country before a search-party could gallop through the gates. Somehow, Taddeo must be distracted.

There was one way. It came to him in a flash of inspiration. A desperate way. But he had been living with the idea of imminent death, and he felt strangely exalted.

It was only a few steps to the menagerie tower. Taddeo and his friends were still some distance away on the far side, laughing and staggering with unsteady legs.

He ran round the corner and snatched the blazing torch from its bracket. He had heard that lions and leopards were frightened by fire. He hoped it was true. He raced through the doorway. The beasts broke into a blood-curdling hubbub. A dozen golden eyes flashed back the torchlight.

He unlatched the door of the first cage and slid it back. For a few heart-stopping moments nothing happened. The leopard made no move to come out. Then, as he backed towards the next cage, and took the intimidating torch with him, the beast was out, a tawny streak, making for the far doorway. Two more cages he stayed to open. Five leopards in all were free. Four, shrinking from the brandished flame, had run spitting and snarling on to the ramparts. One challenged him, ferocious and un-dismayed.

He walked slowly backwards, the torch sketching fiery circles in the air. Sometimes the leopard cringed, padded back a pace or two, tail furiously swishing, then ran for-ward again, relentlessly stalking him. Sandro was dimly aware that a tremendous uproar had broken out on the far side of the tower.

From the corner of his eye he saw now the thick ropes twisted round and round the merlon, securing his own cage. At the next embrasure he would find the ladder dangling. He put out his left hand, his fingertips met the knotted cords. The leopard, sensing that his concentration had momentarily relaxed, sank on its forepaws, ready to spring.

This was the instant of crisis. Life or death. As the baleful eyes narrowed he hurled the torch at them. Then, without waiting to see the effect, he slipped over the wall and swung himself down into the darkness, feet scrabbling for the unseen rungs below.

CHAPTER NINETEEN

Horsemen on the Hills

AFTER that, it was mainly a matter of endurance.

The girls were waiting as he splashed into the moat. "I'm all right," he gasped, then kept his mouth shut as he struck out across the malodorous water. It was lucky that the Castel Sismondo was yet unfinished and there was no sheer wall to scramble up when they reached the other side, only an earth bank on which he could collapse like a stranded fish.

But this was no time to collapse. Quickly he forced himself to his feet. They must get away from the vicinity of the castle while the garrison was kept busy with the ranging leopards. With luck, the rope-ladder would not be noticed, let alone the disappearance of the prisoners, until the beasts were back in their cages or killed. And several hours of darkness still remained.

Somehow, by sunrise, they must reach the comparative safety of the hills. The sky was still clear, the stars shed a faint light. The line of the hills, humped like the backs of huddled sheep, was discernible to the south. They plodded towards them, blundering through spectral or-chards of silvery olive-trees, until they hit a road leading in the direction they wanted. Sandro glanced continually to right and left, watchful for the cover they might need if they heard hoofs behind them.

It was chilly. Their soaked clothing was dank and tight over their bodies. "The food!" said Caterina despairingly. "Oh, Sandro, we kept food, knowing how hungry you'd be. You should have had it before we went into the moat – but everything happened so quickly – and now it will be quite sodden –"

"I couldn't have swallowed a bite till we were safely out of there," he consoled her. "It would have choked me. I shall be all right." But his legs were weak under him, and it was as much as he could do to keep up the pace.

Lucia, behind them, heard this muttered exchange. "Stop," she said. "I have the food. It is quite dry."

They turned in their tracks. Her hands went up to her turban, fumbling. She unwrapped a white napkin. There was the bread and meat Caterina had saved from her dinner, with a few dried figs and olives.

"You are a wonder, Lucia." If they got safely out of this, he told himself, he would see that this girl's future was taken care of. Gratefully he seized on the food. The girls would take only a fig apiece. Lucia produced a small flask of wine from the bosom of her doublet. They passed it round, sipping it in turn. It gave them new heart and took some of the chill out of their bones. Then, Sandro still chewing olives and spitting out the stones as he went, they pressed on again towards the hills.

Sandro was reminded of the night march, a month or two earlier. There was the same momentary paralysis of fear when a village watch-dog gave notice of their passing. But the black girl seemed to have an uncanny premonition of houses in front. Once she had grasped the general direction in which they had to go, she slipped naturally into the lead. The forest craft of her early childhood came to the fore again. It was she who sensed a village ahead, found narrow field-paths for their detour, and then unerringly brought them back to the road again.

All this took time. Speed would have been impossible in any case. By now, at the end of a day and night of strain and without sleep, they were nearing the end of their tether. The rough road, the negotiation of ditches and other obstacles half invisible in the gloom, slowed their pace still further.

In the fields, between the rows of vines or olives, they went in single file, stealthy and unspeaking. Even on the road, where they could walk abreast, their progress was largely wordless, their rare speech limited to the distance they must have covered or had still to go. More than once Caterina's hand sought Sandro's. There would be time later to talk. The pressure of entwined fingers was sufficient communication.

"It's getting light," he said, turning to look back. Over the sea the dawn was beginning to break. Long fingers of gold spread fanwise behind the silhouette of Castel Sismondo, still ominously near.

"I must look a complete buffoon," Caterina said.

The parti-coloured hose clung wrinkled and mud-smeared, one slender leg now recognizably crimson, the other silver grey. Her hair hung lank on the shoulders of a blue tunic too long in the sleeve and too tight across the chest. Her hands were bruised and scraped, her nails broken.

"You look beautiful," he assured her.

The first foothills of the Apennines rose in front of them. They struggled up a stony track, triumphant that the coastal plain was now behind. Pausing for breath, they saw the sun flash from the Adriatic horizon. The mountains ahead of them caught the upward-slanting spears of light.

"Soon be safe," he panted.

Lucia said, "I see horsemen."

She pointed. A mile or two back on the road they had traversed they saw the twinkle of moving steel.

"Come on, then." But he wondered, as they set their faces to the slope, how much longer they could keep going. His own legs were trembling. Caterina looked as though she had had enough. He glanced desperately to right and left. "Perhaps we could hide –"

"Malatesta keeps a pack of hounds in the castle." Lucia stopped and listened intently. Then she came on again, calling. "Yes – I hear. They have the hounds with them."

So it was no use taking cover, even if they found any. They could only drive themselves on. Perhaps they could reach really rough country before their pursuers caught up with them, country too rough for horses, a mountain stream to break the line of scent the hounds were following . . . It was a frail hope.

"It's – no – *good* –" sobbed Caterina, floundering. He saved her from falling and pulled her a few yards further.

He looked back. Even the frail hope was gone. The horsemen, about ten of them, were barely half a mile behind. He could see the hounds still nearer. The leading rider was distinguishable as Taddeo.

To cap everything, there was a cry of despair from the black girl – the first sign she had given, all that time, of losing heart.

"There are horsemen in front as well, sir! They have cut us off!"

He swung round again and stared up at the hillside, suffused in the morning sunshine. Lucia was right. There were horsemen strung along the crest, dozens of them, reined in like so many silver statuettes, motionless, gazing down. A banner streamed like a flame against the sky.

Through parched lips he croaked, "No! Those are the Montefeltro colours!" And even as he stared, the riders on the ridge came to life and began to move down, unwinding like a necklace on the green slope.

He looked back to Taddeo again. He too had seen. The Malatesta riders had halted, clustered. They were pointing upwards. The hounds were being recalled. As Sandro watched, his chest still heaving uncontrollably, he saw the whole party wheel and ride back towards the sea.

"You know, Sandro, you never kept one promise."

"Promise? Which one?"

Federigo chuckled comfortably. "How you rise to a challenge! Don't be so defensive. It was made when we were boys. More than thirty years ago." His one sound eye twinkled as he gave Sandro his familiar side-long smile. Since the wound to his other eye he had developed this habit of turning the same profile, whether he was sitting for his portrait to Piero della Francesca or Justus van Ghent or chatting to an old friend in the privacy of his study.

"Ah! I remember. *You* were to be a famous condottiere – you've certainly kept your promise. *I* was –"

"To accompany me on all my campaigns and write the story of my victories!"

"I did some –"

"But you tired, young Sandro! You should be ashamed. And I three years your senior."

Sandro laughed. "You have had too many campaigns, too many victories. You are Knight of the Ermine, Knight of the Golden Rose – even the distant English know your name, and their King makes you Knight of the Garter. You hardly needed my pen to sing your praises."

"Oh, nobody could tell a tall story as well as you."

Federigo rubbed his broken nose with a reflective gesture. "And I always admired your turn of phrase. You deserted me."

"Nonsense – with respect, my lord Duke!" Sandro echoed his mockery. "I was with you in every fight against Malatesta –"

"Granted –"

"But Malatesta was broken long ago – he's been in his grave these six years, now. I was more use to you here while this palace was building. Your 'castle in the air', remember? That was another promise you kept. Then you wanted my help with the library –"

"You did a good job," Federigo admitted. Lovingly he stroked the crimson binding of the Petrarch on the table in front of him. "Though we have still to finish it. I shan't be happy till we have a perfect copy of every book written, whether it's in Latin or Greek or Hebrew."

"No rest, ever!"

Federigo stood up. "Time to join our families in the loggia. It is a pleasant place to sit, these summer evenings, looking out upon the mountains."

"Caterina and I have built something similar – on not so grand a scale – at San Stefano. Lucia calls it our golden birdcage!"

"I must come to see it." Federigo put the book tenderly under his arm and led the way through the palace to where the others were waiting in the loggia. "Caterina," he mused. "I used to think she was an odd girl. Once I even suspected her of trying to poison me."

"You never told me that!"

"It wouldn't have been fair. I realised afterwards that her motives were –" Federigo coughed – "quite different. You know, poor Taddeo Tregani, God rest his spotted soul, did you a good turn, without meaning to."

"Don't I know it? I've never ceased to thank Heaven. That kidnapping finished the Sorbolo engagement. If her father hadn't been desperate to find her a husband of some sort, he'd never have accepted a nobody like me."

"You overlook dear Caterina. I think Caterina would always have got what *she* wanted, in the end. But I fancy the affair at Rimini did a lot to clarify her mind."

They had reached the loggia. It was glowing with the sunset. The creamy Dalmatian limestone of the new palace gleamed rosy. The others sat contemplating the rooftops of Urbino at their feet and the amphitheatre of darkening mountains beyond. They rose like a flock of birds to greet their duke.

"Ah, Caterina!" Federigo kissed her hand. "More beautiful than ever! I was telling your Sandro how lucky he was."

"I am the lucky one, Federigo. What have you been reading? Petrarch?"

"Yes. I found some wise words I would like to read out to your grandchildren."

"Please."

Federigo opened the silver clasps, found the right page, and focussed his eye on the vellum page. With quiet emphasis he began to read aloud: "'*One is not born noble, one becomes noble* ...'"

"That is very true," said Caterina softly.

Behind her back, unseen by the rest of them, her hand groped for Sandro's and found it.

Author's Note

ANY reader with a passion for detecting historical discrepancies may be able to find examples of minor liberties taken with the dating of events in this story, though in all other respects it conscientiously follows the known facts regarding the Gonzagas of Mantua, Vittorino's school, and the lives of Federigo da Montefeltro and Sigismondo Malatesta. A casual perusal of the relevant chapter in the author's own historical study, *The Condottieri*, will show that these small discrepancies are just as obvious to him and quite deliberate. Caterina's town of San Stefano will be found on no map, but the story of its recapture is based closely on that of San Leo, one of the earliest of Federigo's actual exploits.

Colwall, January, 1971.   G.T.